The Tamarack Murders

The Tamarack Murders

A Bo Tully Mystery

by
Patrick F. McManus

Skyhorse Publishing

Skyhorse Publishing books may be purchased in bulk at special discounts for sales promotion, corporate gifts, fund-raising, or educational purposes. Special editions can also be created to specifications. For details, contact the Special Sales Department, Skyhorse Publishing, 307 West 36th Street, 11th Floor, New York, NY 10018 or info@skyhorsepublishing.com.

Visit our website at www.skyhorsepublishing.com.

10 9 8 7 6 5 4 3 2 1

Library of Congress Cataloging-in-Publication Data is available on file.

Cover design by Adam Bozarth

Print ISBN: 978-1-63220-680-0
Ebook ISBN: 978-1-62636-861-3

Printed in the United States of America

Chapter 1

Blight County Idaho Sheriff Bo Tully scanned the ridge above him. A string of six elk trotted over it next to the vertical column of rock that served as the peak and namesake of Chimney Rock Mountain. The elk moved diagonally down the slope away from him. Something had spooked them, probably hunters. It was the third day of elk season. The fall's first snow had dusted the ridge white. Tully automatically recorded the number of points on the bull's rack. Eight. A royal. The bull followed the line of five cows, in case they could be headed for danger.

Tully wasn't hunting elk. He was hunting a man. A person anyway. He should have been hunting elk. Anyone with a halfway decent job would have been hunting elk. He signaled to Deputy Brian Pugh to move up the slope. Pugh shook his head and pointed up the mountain and off to their left. Tully leaned around the tree in front of him and caught a movement fifty yards up. It might be Deputy Ernie Thorpe. He looked back down the slope. Thorpe was below him, standing next to a cedar stump gray with age and the size of a small house.

Tully pointed in the direction of the movement he had just seen. Thorpe nodded. He slowly and quietly jacked a shell into the chamber of his rifle. He had seen the movement too. Tully shook his head. Thorpe nodded again. The movement above Tully could have been made by a hunter. He didn't want anyone killed today, including the bank robber. Or one of his deputies. Typically, bank robbers were desperate rather than greedy or simply lazy. Desperate didn't rule out greedy or lazy, but it made them more dangerous.

He checked his wristwatch. Ten thirty-five.

As Tully watched, a man stepped from behind a large tamarack, the tree bright yellow and glowing in the morning sun as if on fire. He wore a black overcoat that stood out sharply against the bright yellow of fallen tamarack needles on the steep slope of the mountain. Not the attire of a hunter or of a bank robber either, for that matter. Fifty yards above the man, the trees thickened into a dense patch of woods, mostly tamarack mixed with evergreens. If the man made it to the woods, he might get away. Tully glanced over at Pugh. The deputy nodded, indicating he had seen the man. He patted his chest, indicating the man could be armed with a handgun. Tully stepped out from behind the tree and shouted. "Hold it, pardner! We've got you covered! Take another step and you're dead!"

The man seemed to sag. He turned and held his arms out to the side, apparently to show he didn't have a weapon.

The shot came from the woods higher on the mountain. It slammed the man face-down on the ground. Tully glanced at Pugh. The deputy shook his head. Thorpe had climbed up behind Tully. "It wasn't me, boss."

Tully shouted at Pugh. "Stay under cover!"

Pugh nodded.

Thorpe said, "Who shot him, Bo?"

"Don't have a clue. Could be a hunter. But the guy certainly doesn't look much like an elk. You never can tell. Idiots hunt too." Tully thought hunting license applications should state, "Put an x in the square if you are an idiot."

"What shall we do?" Thorpe asked

"I don't know, Ernie." Tully felt short of breath even though he hadn't moved for ten minutes. "I don't want any of us killed too."

"It could be some freelance vigilante," Thorpe said.

"Yeah, but how would he know this guy had just robbed a bank?" he yelled at Pugh. "You and Ernie cover me, Brian. I'm going to go up and check on the guy."

Pugh yelled back, "I don't think that's such a good idea, boss!"

"You're right, Pugh. You go!"

"It was your idea, boss!"

Tully stepped out from behind the tree and moved up toward the body. There were plenty of people around who wouldn't mind killing him, and he hoped whoever shot the man wasn't one of them. He watched the woods for any sign of movement. He had long ago taught himself to see in past the tree line. If anything moved in there, he was ready to drop flat on the rocky surface of the slope and hope that Pugh and Thorpe missed him when they laid down a covering fire. For a second he thought he heard the sound of a motor on the other side of the ridge, but he knew there wasn't a road over there. The shooter could have retreated up the ridge behind the cover of trees and then escaped on an all-terrain vehicle of some kind.

Tully came to the body. It was lying straight down the slope on its stomach. The shot had hit him squarely between the shoulder blades. Blood soaked through the back of the black overcoat. He wore slacks, a white shirt, and gray wool, knitted gloves with leather faces, possibly to warm his hands but more likely to keep from leaving fingerprints in the car. The coat and slacks were weirdly out of place up here on the mountainside, to say nothing of the white shirt. The shoes were shiny black oxfords, well-worn and no doubt polished numerous times. Not great shoes for climbing a steep mountain slope. He appeared to be fairly young, no more than late twenties. Tully pulled on a pair of of latex gloves, knelt down and went through his pockets. Nothing. Neither was there a bag of bank money anywhere in sight. He began to get the uneasy feeling this wasn't the bank robber. He took out his phone and called the office. His secretary, Daisy Quinn, answered.

"Daisy, we're out here above Canyon Creek Road on the side of Chimney Rock Mountain. A man's just been shot and killed."

"Oh no!"

"Not one of us, Daisy, and we didn't do it. I don't know who it is or who did it. We think it's the guy who robbed the bank, but there's no sign of the loot. He left the getaway car in the ditch and started climbing the mountain. We'd been in pursuit of the car and got here a few minutes later. Three department Explorers are parked around the vehicle so even our people can't miss it. Right now we're a quarter way up the mountain. I need the Unit up here."

By "Unit" he meant his Crime Scene Investigations Unit, namely one Byron Proctor, possibly the homeliest man in the world but also one of the smartest. Tully had nicknamed him Lurch.

"You got it, boss," Daisy said. "I'll get him on his way." Tully beeped off and dialed the medical examiner's office. The secretary answered.

"Ginny, this is Sheriff Tully. Is Susan in?"

"Yes, Sheriff, but right at the moment she's busy doing a—"

"Skip the gory details, Ginny. Just get the M.E. on the phone."

A moment passed. He could hear a door open and close. Susan came on. "Hi, Bo. What's up?

"I'm on the side of a Chimney Rock Mountain off Canyon Creek Road. We've got a shooting vic here, probably a bank robber."

"Dead?"

"That's my guess. His chest is practically blown away."

"That's usually a clue. How do I find you?"

He told her. "You can't miss it. There are three red department Ford Explorers parked near a car in the ditch."

"We'll be right out."

"Call Lurch, Susan, and tell him you'll pick him up. He's throwing his CSI kit together. Tell him to bring his metal detector. Maybe he can find the bullet that killed the guy."

"Got it, Bo." She hung up.

Tully motioned for Pugh and Thorpe to join him. The deputies moved cautiously up the slope, both of them watching the grove of trees. Pugh came up next to Tully, looked down at the body, and shook his head. "Guy seems pretty young and clean-cut to be robbing banks."

"Yeah, that's what I thought," Tully said. "I guess bank robbers don't come in a type that fits all."

Thorpe came up, his rifle at the ready.

Tully frowned at him. "If you don't mind, Ernie, click that safety back on. It's too early in the day to get my head blown off, not to mention some other valued part."

"Sorry, boss." Thorpe clicked the safety on.

"Keep an eye on those trees up there, Ernie. I think our shooter is long gone but just in case."

"Right, boss."

Tully turned to Pugh. "Brian, you've hunted this mountain. What's on the other side of the ridge up there?"

"Another mountain. The other side of the ridge drops off steep down into Rattle Creek Canyon. It's a real hellhole down there, great tangles of brush and downed trees with the crick running through the whole mess. Elk love it."

"I imagine. Did you see that little herd cross over a bit ago?"

Pugh laid his rifle down on the tamarack needles, jammed his hands in his pockets, shuddered, and hunched his shoulders against the cold. "Yeah, that was a nice royal bringing up the rear. Something must have spooked them out of Rattle Creek. I figured we'd hear some shooting from where they were headed down the mountain. But nothing."

Tully took out his phone and dialed Daisy. "Good point, Brian. I'll keep that in mind."

Daisy answered. "Sheriff's office."

"Daisy, see if you can get ahold of Dave Perkins over in Famine. He's probably at his restaurant."

"Dave's House of Fry?"

"Yeah, try there first. Tell him I need a tracker over here pronto. I'll meet him at my car which he can't miss if he takes the Canyon Creek Road." He beeped off.

Tully slid the phone into his pocket and turned to Pugh. "I thought I heard a motor on the other side of the ridge a few minutes ago."

Pugh gazed up at the ridge. "I don't think so, boss. There's no road over there, just an old a pack trail of sorts. I think maybe outfitters used it years ago as a mule trail to supply that Forest Service lookout up on that far peak."

Tully squinted at the distant tower, a tiny speck perched on a massive slab of rock. Some of its wraparound windows glistened in the sun. "The Forest Service kept that one and a few others but burned down most of the towers. I think they rent what's left to people who want a wilderness vacation over the summer." He turned his attention to the ridge. "You think an ATV could make it up that old pack trail, Brian?"

"Maybe. It would be a rough ride, though. Why?"

"The guy who killed our friend here, that's about the only way he could get away. Do you know who owns this property?"

"Nope. There's never been any No Trespassing signs on it, so I figure it's okay to hunt here. Could be state land."

Tully squinted at the ridge. The dusting of snow along it was the first snow of the season. "Now here's what I want you two guys to do."

"I hate to hear this," Thorpe said.

"Me too," Pugh said. "It's not as if we're dressed for this cold, boss." His breath misted in the air.

"Quit whining," Tully said. "We could get a lot of snow any day now and all sign would be wiped out. There's already a skiff of snow along the ridge. There might be some tracks in it if the shooter crossed through the snow. He had to get off the mountain some way. You two go up there and see what you can find. Be careful where you step. I've got the tracker coming in, and he gets upset if we disturb anything."

"Maybe you should hire Dave full time," Pugh said.

"Hiring Dave would be too expensive. This way he works for nothing."

"Dave Perkins is rich off that restaurant of his anyway," Thorpe said. "He's probably killed more people with his House of Fry's chicken-fried steaks than all the murderers we've put in prison."

Tully smiled. "And they're not the only ones he's killed. If you find any kind of evidence, leave it for Lurch and Dave. Lurch knows how to make casts out of even tracks in snow."

Pugh shivered and stared up at the ridge. "What if we freeze to death while we're waiting for Lurch and the tracker?"

"We'll give you really nice funerals. Dave won't be here until afternoon. You'd definitely freeze if I made you wait for him."

"You're going soft, boss," Thorpe said. The two deputies slogged off toward the ridge.

Tully watched them go, then broke some small dead branches off the tamarack, made a little teepee of them, and held the flame of his pipe lighter to them. Although he no longer smoked, he still carried the lighter for just such occasions. As the flames leaped up the teepee he added more twigs and finally some dead branches. Soon he was squatted down warming his hands over the fire. He could hear the distant sirens of approaching emergency vehicles. Rubbing his hands together over the fire, he glanced at the dead man. "Too bad one of us didn't think to bring sausages." The tamarack was sprinkling the body with needles, turning it bright yellow.

His radio squawked. It was Thorpe. "We found some tracks crossing the skiff of snow, boss! Just one set coming up from below."

"Great, Ernie! The Unit is on his way. Mark the tracks so we know they probably belong to the shooter. I'll send Lurch up as soon as he gets here."

He dialed the office again. "Daisy, call the State Patrol. Ask them to have their officers check any cars headed out of Blight County on the main highways, particularly those towing an all-terrain vehicle. Get IDs for passengers and drivers. Tell them the guys we're after are dangerous, that they've robbed a bank and murdered a man."

Daisy asked, "How long do you want the State Patrol checking cars?"

"A couple of hours. After that we'll know the bad guys are hiding in the county somewhere. One last thing. Send out a wrecker to tow the getaway car into the department garage. I'll send Lurch back in with it." He beeped off.

His radio squawked. It was Pugh. "We found only that one set of tracks crossing the skiff of snow, boss."

"Good, Brian. Those tracks have to be from the shooter. The Unit is on his way. Make sure he makes casts of the right tracks. I'll send him right up. You find anything else?"

"Yeah. There are all-terrain-vehicle tracks in the snow going down the trail. None coming up. That's probably the motor you heard. In a bare spot next to a tree we can see the ATV tracks both coming up and going down. They show up in the dirt pretty clear."

Tully thought for a moment. "That's weird. If the shooter drove the ATV in, that means he had to get here before the snow."

"Sounds about right," Pugh said. "The only human track in the snow is the one coming up the mountain. Except for ours that is."

Tully beeped off and put another broken branch on his fire. "Boss?" It was Thorpe on the radio. "Can we head back down now?"

"Pretty soon, Ernie. I hear some sirens. The M.E. and her people are on the way. I take it you didn't find any evidence of the shooter in the woods."

"Nothing, boss. Not so much as a gum wrapper."

"Okay, you and Thorpe come on down."

Chapter 2

The medical examiner and the Unit plodded up the slope followed by two of Susan's assistants carrying a folded stretcher between then. Susan lugged two of her black M.E. cases, with her tan shoulder bag bouncing and twisting. He knew she carried a gun in the bag. Lurch had brought his metal detector. Both Susan and Lurch were panting when they got to him. Susan dropped both her kits on the ground and squatted next to the fire, holding her hands over the flames. "Looks like a picnic," she said.

"Aside from the fact I'm half frozen," Tully said. He nodded at the corpse. "My friend here is in even worse shape."

"I can see that. It's almost beautiful. A bright-yellow corpse. Looks almost like one of those gold statues they find in Egyptian pyramids." She turned the body up on its side. "Wow! You're right. He was hit really hard!"

"Can't be hit much harder," Tully said.

She lowered the body. "You think it was a hunting accident?"

"Could be, but he was standing in an open area, and the shot came from that patch of woods up there." He pointed. "As you can see, he looks nothing like an elk. I have no doubt he was killed on purpose."

"You get a line on the shot?" the Unit asked.

"Yeah. It knocked him straight down the slope. Sight along the body, Lurch, and that should give you the line. The bullet came from a big-bore rifle, no doubt about that. The bullet may have gone almost down to the road."

The Unit groaned. "Great! I just climbed up from there."

"Stop whining, Lurch. By the way, take some photos of the body while you're here, before Susan starts messing with it."

Susan put her hands on her hips and glared at him. "I'm not messing with it! I assume you can give me the exact time of death, Bo."

"That I can. I checked my watch just before he was shot. Ten thirty-five."

She wrote the time in her notebook. "That saves you from some of my messing."

"Good. I would have lied if necessary, but I happened to check my watch just before he was shot."

Susan shook her head and stashed the notebook back in her shoulder bag.

Lurch took a dozen photos of the body and the surrounding scene.

"Good enough, Lurch," Tully said. "Now see if you can find that bullet, because afterwards I need you to hike up to the ridge."

"Wonderful!"

The two attendants rolled the body onto the stretcher, covered it with a sheet, and strapped it down.

"Not much I can do here," Susan said. "We'll head on in. Better put some more wood on your fire."

Tully's radio squawked.

"That's probably Pugh," he told Susan. "Maybe he's found something." He pressed a button on his radio. "Yeah, Pugh."

"We're ready to head down, boss."

"Wait! Lurch will be up there shortly."

Tully turned and yelled down the slope. "Hurry up, Lurch. I've got another job for you."

He spoke into his radio. "Brian, I'm sending the Unit up right now. Point out the tracks you want him to cast. Oh, I just remembered something. Have Lurch shoot some photos of the elk tracks over by Chimney Rock. They're right next to the rock."

"You got it, boss! Tell Lurch to get the lead out. I'm sending Ernie down. His chattering teeth are getting on my nerves."

Susan smiled and shook her head. The two attendants hoisted the stretcher and started carrying the body down to the road. Susan followed. Below them, Tully could see the Unit squatted down and brushing the ground. He held something up.

"I got it, boss!"

"Great, Lurch! Now get back up here!"

"I was going to check the car!" the Unit yelled.

"No!" Tully yelled back. "Check it later! You go up and see what Thorpe and Pugh found and take pictures of everything! Make a cast of all tracks in the snow and dirt that don't belong to Thorpe or Pugh! Photograph any you can't cast!"

Going down, Tully met the Unit as he slogged back up the mountain. Lurch handed him a tiny white envelope with a hard lump inside. "Looks like seven millimeter, boss. Hollow point."

"Good work, Lurch. From the damage to the vic, that's what I expected. I'm going to check out the car, but I want you to go over it for prints when you get it back to the department garage. Now head straight up through the grove of trees and you'll run into Pugh and Thorpe on the other side of the ridge. Pugh says he's found some ATV tracks over there. I'm pretty sure the shooter took out our vic from a spot somewhere in the patch of woods. See if you can find any sign of him in there. If you do, leave it for the tracker."

Lurch smiled and nodded. "Right, boss."

"Shoot some pictures of the ATV tracks. I hope you've got some of that stuff you spray into the snow so you can make casts of the shooter's tracks?"

"Right, boss. Snow wax, a clear acrylic hardening spray. It hardens the snow before I pour in the plaster."

"Excellent. The bullet, footprints, and ATV tracks may be the only evidence we have of the shooter. I'll wait for you in my car."

"Be careful, boss. You don't want to catch cold."

"Get going, Lurch, or you may have to walk back to town."

A breeze had come up and seemed to push the chill all the way through to Tully's bones. He tried flapping his arms, but the effort failed to warm him. He continued on down the mountain.

He stopped at the getaway car to look it over. The driver's door was wedged against the high inside bank of the ditch. The driver would have had to climb out on the passenger side. Since the victim was wearing gloves when he was shot, he probably had been wearing them driving the car. Not much chance of Lurch finding useful prints. Odd, the victim didn't appear to be the kind of person who knew how to steal a car. One thing about car thieves, they tend to look the part. And they don't bother stealing vehicles on their last legs, or tires, as the case may be. There was only one reason for robbers to steal a car this old. He wrapped his hand in his handkerchief, opened the right front door and reached in far enough to grab the ignition key and pull it out. He checked the grooves in it, then shoved the key back into the ignition. Strange thing for bank robbers to use. You had to wiggle a shaved key around until it engaged with the right grooves and turned on the ignition. He couldn't imagine robbers rushing out to their getaway car and wiggling a key around to get the old thing started and their escape underway. The key suddenly caught the right groves and the car sputtered to life. He shut it off. He looked up through the windshield. A length of orange flagging tape dangled from a tree branch directly in front of the car. Odd that the car would be dumped right by the tape. He walked back to his Explorer, started the engine and let it warm up while he waited for Lurch. Once the car was comfortable he shut off the engine and dozed. He awoke just in time to see the Unit trudging off the mountain with his CSI kit. Lurch opened the hatch door of the Explorer, set his kit in the cargo space, and closed the door. He walked around and opened the passenger door. "I got casts of the tracks, boss, both from the ATV and what must be those of the shooter when he went up through the snow. Can I ride back to town with you?" He held his hands out toward the cold heater. "Pugh and Thorpe are on their way down."

Tully started the engine and the heater began to blow out warm air on Lurch's hands. He said, "I'm waiting for the tracker to show up. Pugh and Thorpe should be down any minute, but I want you to ride back with the wrecker, just to make sure nobody gets inside the getaway car and messes up anything. Check for prints when you get it back to the department garage. Now go cut down that piece of flagging tape. There's something odd about its being right where our vic dumped the car."

"You suppose the flagging tape will last until I thaw out my hands, boss?"

"No! You're such a wuss, Lurch. Be careful when you cut it down, because there should be some fingerprints on it. Don't add any."

The Unit sighed, pulled on latex gloves, got out, walked over and grabbed the tip of the tape, pulled it down until he could reach the branch and break it off. Holding the tape by the edge, he rolled it up, put a rubber band around it and walked to the back of the Explorer, opened one of his CSI kits, put the tape in a clear plastic envelope and sealed it. After climbing back into the passenger seat next to Tully, he bent over, removed his latex gloves and put his hands practically on the heater.

Tully shook his head. "You definitely are a wuss, Lurch. But you're in luck. Here comes the tow truck to haul the getaway car to the department garage.

But I just thought of something. A herd of elk walked through right up next to chimney rock. I need close-up photos of those tracks."

"Ha! I've already got them, boss! Pugh told me to shoot them. What do elk tracks have to do with this killing anyway?"

"I don't know, but I'll think of something."

Chapter 3

Dave Perkins drove up next to Tully's car shortly after noon. Tully walked over to Dave's big white pickup truck and climbed in beside him. "About time you got here."

Dressed in wool pants, a thick wool shirt, a lambskin coat, and lambskin hat, the tracker was sliding his hands into matching lambskin mittens. Tully thought it would be a good idea for the county to buy its sheriff a similar outfit, if he had to investigate any more crimes out in the cold.

Dave said, "As always, the minute I got Daisy's call I dropped everything and walked out the door. Nevermind that my restaurant goes to pieces while I'm gone. Anyway, about our murder, I just hope you and your people haven't messed up the murder scene so much that finding the killer will be impossible."

"The murder scene is pristine, Sherlock. So find me the killer."

"Then let's get to it, Watson."

Tully led the tracker up to where the shape of the body had been marked off in yellow crime-scene tape. Lurch had placed rocks on the tape to hold it down.

"Our victim was hit right here," Tully said. "The shot came from up there in the woods. Pugh and Thorpe were with me when he got hit. Knocked him flat, straight downhill. The hollow point came from a big-bore rifle. Turned out to be a seven millimeter. Hit the vic in the back and practically blew away his chest. My theory is he was shot to keep him quiet about his accomplices in the robbery and maybe to glomb his share of the loot. Even if we hadn't been hot on his heels, I think he would have been shot."

Tully told Dave about the flagging tape that marked the spot where the getaway car was dumped in the ditch. He pointed toward the woods. "I'm pretty sure the shooter was up there waiting for him. The kid probably thought the tape marked the spot for him to make his getaway. Instead, it marked the spot for him to get killed."

Dave studied the woods. "How about the loot?"

"Gone. No sign of it."

As they came to the wooded area, Dave turned and ask if Tully was sure the shot had come from there.

"Had to be," Tully said. "It knocked the victim flat and straight downhill. The shooter had to be directly above him."

"Sounds about right." Dave turned and looked back at the spot where the victim had fallen. He scanned the ground ahead of him as the two of them moved slowly up through the woods.

"Nothing," Tully said.

The tracker turned and smiled. "Not exactly." He took Tully by the arm, led him back down through the woods, and pointed to a couple of small indents in the tamarack needles, tiny mounds of black dirt pushed up from them. "The killer made a sitting shot from right here, his arms braced on his knees to steady the rifle. Or it could have been a pistol, if the guy is a terrific shot. The little mounds of dirt are where his heels dug into the ground."

Tully shook his head in amazement. "You're right! Why didn't I see that! Even worse, why didn't Lurch see it?"

"Because you and Lurch aren't trackers," Dave said. "If you look carefully you'll see where the shooter's rear end made an impression in the needles."

Tully stared. "I see it! You're amazing, Dave! I think I'll get Lurch up here to make a cast."

Dave laughed. "Does the FBI keep a collection of rear-end impressions?"

"Probably."

"Think they would make one of Angie's for me?"

"I doubt it. They probably have a rule against catering to perverts. I wouldn't be surprised if Angie is sent back here to investigate the bank robbery though."

"In that case it may take several days for me to unravel this mystery for you, Watson."

"How did I ever guess that, Holmes? I suppose now you might even want to be paid."

"That would be refreshing."

They made their way up to the ridge, without Dave indicating any more signs. When they reached the skiff of snow, Tully walked in Dave's tracks. He told

Dave, "Lurch made casts of the only set of tracks that didn't belong to him, Brian, or Ernie."

The three deputies had marked their own tracks with twigs, and Lurch, presumably, had taped notes to the twigs identifying the tracks of each deputy.

Dave pointed to the ATV tracks in the bare ground under the overhang of a tree, one coming up and the other going down. "Interesting," he said.

"Really?" Tully said.

"Yeah." Dave squatted down and examined each track where it crossed through the bare dirt. "From what you told me, I assumed an accomplice had driven an ATV up the trail and picked up the shooter."

"That's what I thought," Tully said.

"If you look at the two tracks closely you'll see there was only one rider coming up and one rider going down."

Tully squatted down to examine the two tracks. "And your reasoning is?"

"Quite simple, Watson. If the ATV had one rider coming up and two riders going down, the two-rider track would leave a deeper impression."

Tully thought about this. "On the other hand, Holmes, suppose two riders came up and two riders went down. Wouldn't the two tracks be of the same depth?"

Dave rubbed his chin thoughtfully. "Yes, Watson, but I had already taken that into account." He pointed. "That set of tracks in the snow is where Ernie came up and that set is where he went down. This other set is where Brian came up and over there is where he went down. The third set over here is where Lurch came up and that is where he went down. We are left with only one other track, the one coming up. The shooter had to come in from the road below or from up here before the snowfall. If he came in from below, he had to be dropped off on the road by someone. If he rode the ATV up, he would have had to come in before the snowfall and had a long cold wait for the target to show up. My guess, he was dropped off on the road before the robbery, climbed up to the grove of trees and waited until his intended target started to climb the mountain, then shot him. That's why there's a track coming up, but none going down through the snow. The shooter escaped on the ATV. He probably brought it in the night before, then walked down the mountain to be picked up on the road."

Tully squatted down to study the tracks. "Sounds about right. You got any idea how many people might be involved in the robbery?"

The tracker thought for a moment. "My guess is a minimum of three, counting your dead guy. Could be a fourth. Your victim probably brought the ATV in the night before. That way he would know the ATV was up here for him to escape on. Unless he was totally stupid, he wouldn't leave his means of escape to somebody else. If in fact the victim was totally stupid, maybe the shooter brought the ATV in the night before, walked down the mountain and was picked up on the road. The shooter seems to be the kind of guy who would want to be sure of his means of escape."

Tully stood up and stretched. "So what happened to the loot from the bank?"

The tracker scratched his jaw. "Let's see now, one of the robbers got shot, but he didn't have the loot."

"That's right," Tully said. "There wasn't any sign of the haul from the bank."

"The shooter wasn't a participant in the robbery itself. Otherwise, he couldn't get in position quick enough to shoot the victim. The victim didn't have the loot. The robbers leave the bank with their ill-gotten gains. So somewhere between the bank and the ditched getaway car the loot had to get handed off. It couldn't get handed off to the shooter, because he would be waiting for the victim up on the mountain. That means there has to be at least one other person involved in the robbery."

Tully thought about this. "You think there was a hand-off?"

"Had to be, don't you think, Bo?"

"Yeah, the loot went somewhere. I suppose the actual bank robber could have jumped out of the getaway car and into a vehicle left along the road and driven off with it and the loot. Now you mention a handoff, Dave, there was an old farm pickup pulled over to the edge of the road, apparently to get out of the way of the pursuit vehicles. Looked like a farmer in the driver's seat and some bales of hay in the bed. The reason I noticed the truck at all, I almost ran into it."

Dave stroked his chin, apparently turning something over in his mind. "So let's say we have three guys involved in the robbery. Two of them come roaring out of town in the getaway car, skid to a stop by the pickup, one of them jumps out with the loot, leaps into the truck and starts it. The driver takes off. After the pursuit vehicles go by, the driver of the pickup pulls out and heads in the direction of town. He meets up with the shooter at some prearranged location, maybe where the pack trail comes down off the mountain. What's your guess, Bo?"

"Sounds workable. I still prefer a fourth robber sitting in the pickup alongside the road with the motor running. That way the first robber could leap into the bed of the pickup and be out of sight in no time. This sounds so good maybe we should take up bank robbing."

Dave laughed. "It's tempting, Bo, but I'm much too old for that kind of business. Might be fun though."

He was silent for a moment. "You know for certain the victim was one of the robbers?"

"He was climbing the hill above the getaway car, which was no doubt stolen. It's an old Datson with a shaved key in the ignition."

"Shaved key, you say?"

"Yeah."

Dave took off his sheepskin hat and scratched his head. "In that case, unless all these guys were total amateurs, they left a guy in the getaway car to keep it running. No one robs a bank and then starts wiggling a key to make his escape. Guy number one robs the bank, guy number two keeps the getaway car running. Guy number three is waiting on the mountain to shoot guy number two."

"Right," Tully said. "And if there is a guy number four, he's waiting in the handoff vehicle to drive away with the loot and the guy who robbed the bank. Looks to me as if there has to be a fourth guy. He's the one taking the least risk. So I suspect he's the mastermind behind the whole robbery."

He pointed toward the large chimney-shaped rock that formed the peak of the mountain. " I have one more set of tracks over there I want you to look at, Dave, before I'm frozen solid."

He led the tracker over to Chimney Rock and showed him the elk tracks. "You make out anything significant from them?"

Dave laughed. "I'm enjoying this way too much. For a brief moment I even thought about not charging the county for my services."

Tully said, "Yeah, a very brief moment I bet. So, anything you can tell me about those tracks?"

Dave squatted and took a close look. "Well, one of the elk was a lot larger than the others, the last in the line, a big bull. I'd guess a royal."

Tully smiled and shook his head. "Okay, okay, you passed the test. Dave, you are absolutely amazing!"

Dave laughed. "Quite so, Watson, quite so. Furthermore, the tracks also tell me that a herd of deer passed through here sometime before the elk. The elk trampled most of the deer tracks, but I can still make out a few of them. In fact, the snow was still falling when the deer went through. The few deer tracks I can make out have only a bit of fresh snow in them. So the snow stopped shortly after they went through. Any significance to the deer tracks?"

"None I can think of."

"How about the elk tracks?"

Tully shoved his hands deep into his pant's pockets in an effort to thaw out his fingers. "I guess the tracks show I didn't imagine the herd of elk."

Dave said, "Well, now that I've solved your robbery and murder for you, I guess I'll head back to the House of Fry."

Tully tugged on the corner of his mustache. "I must have missed something, Dave. Who did you say the robbers were and where I can find them and the loot?"

"Details, details. I'll leave those to you, Bo. You're the sheriff."

Chapter 4

Tully met the Unit in the courthouse parking lot, and they walked back to the office together.

Lurch told him that the M.E. had lifted the victim's prints, and he had just picked them up. "If the owner of them has any kind of record, I should be able to get you some identification on him."

"Great, Lurch. That'll give us a start anyway."

Florence, the radio person, stuck her head out of her office as they walked in. "I just made a fresh pot, boss, and filled your coffee pump."

"Thanks, Flo. Don't know what I'd do without you."

Lurch frowned at her. "How about me, Flo?"

She smiled. "I don't have to suck up to you, Lurch. See what's left in the troop pumps."

Tully greeted Daisy Quinn and was rewarded with a nice smile before she went back to her computer. Lurch followed him into his glassed-in office and slid into a chair across the desk from Tully, who had flopped into his office swivel chair. "How about the flagging tape, Lurch? You get the prints off of it?"

The Unit laughed. "You expect me to have checked the tape already?"

"Yeah. What did you find?"

"You're unbelievable, boss."

"That's what people tell me. So what did you find?"

"One partial print."

Tully frowned. "One partial? That's odd. How could a person cut off a piece of flagging tape and tie it to a limb without getting more than one partial print on it?"

"Maybe he wore gloves," Lurch said, rocking his chair back against the sheriff's steel gun safe. "Maybe he wiped the tape for prints?"

Tully stared at him. "Who wears gloves to put up flagging tape? Who wipes it for prints?"

"I guess someone who doesn't want his prints found on it," Lurch said. "Even though I got only the partial, it was enough for me to get a match."

"No kidding! You got an ID!"

"Yep, one Gridley Shanks, who lives out on Route 2, about five miles from town. He doesn't have much of a record, but he was once arrested for beating three bikers senseless. Charges were later dismissed when witnesses reported he had been attacked first. He was carrying a concealed weapon at the time of his arrest, but he had a permit. There was no record it had ever been used in a crime. The gun was returned to Shanks after the charges were dismissed."

"Beat up three bikers! They must have been the kind of bikers who pedal."

Lurch shook his head. "Nope, the other kind. He's apparently a formidable individual."

"And this Shanks belongs to the partial print?"

"Right."

Daisy came and stood in the doorway. "So, boss, we've got another murder on our hands, not to mention a bank robbery?"

"Afraid so." Lurch gave Daisy his chair and went back to work.

Tully took a sip of his coffee, eyeing Daisy over the top of it. They had concluded a messy affair a few weeks before, but she seemed back to her same perky self—white shiny blouse, short tight black skirt, curly black hair bobbed short, a very compact and cute little number.

Daisy said, "Somebody should call in a stolen vehicle report on the getaway car, don't you think?"

Tully shook his head. "Probably not on this car. The owner is no doubt glad to be rid of it. It was easy pickings for the guy who boosted it."

"You don't think the victim stole it?"

"Maybe. But he doesn't look like a car thief."

"I didn't know car thieves had a special look."

"It's more that people who don't boost cars have a look. And the vic had that look. Anything else going on?"

Daisy consulted her pad. "This should be of interest to you. Your fortune-teller is back in town."

"You're kidding! Etta is back?"

"Yes indeed. She wants you to give her a call."

He studied Daisy for signs of irritation, found none. She was an ace secretary. So much so, he had promoted her to deputy and issued her a department gun, a .38-cal. revolver. On the target range, at least, Daisy could now outshoot all the deputies except Pugh. On the other hand, Etta Gorsich, perhaps ten years older than Daisy, could make his heart stop merely by putting her hand on his chest.

Daisy stared at him. "What's wrong, boss?"

He didn't want to say he was involved with too many women. "Nothing. It's just that we've got this weird case. I have no doubt our shooting vic is one of the bank robbers, but we haven't found the loot. He wasn't carrying it when we tracked him up the mountain. There was no place for him to hide it. And there was no gun. He was like a decoy."

"That's weird," Daisy said. "How much did the bank say he got away with?"

"I don't know. I suspect the FBI is all over it by now."

"You bet," Daisy said. "They've got half a dozen agents on it. Flew them in. Guess who one of them is."

"I have no idea."

"Your little friend, Angela Phelps!"

Tully started to smile but caught himself in time. "Oh no, not her!"

"I know she can't be as bad as you let on, boss."

Tully shook his head. "She's a whole lot worse than I let on, Daisy. I'm a person of great restraint when it comes to Angie Phelps."

"Well, she's the SAC."

"Angie's the special agent in charge? I guess she's moving up in the bureau. Probably picked up a lot of investigative techniques from me."

"She no doubt picked up a lot of techniques from you, boss, but you were probably doing most of the investigating."

"Very funny. Now beat it, Daisy. I've got to make some phone calls."

Daisy grinned as she gently shut the door behind her.

Tully grabbed the phone book and looked up the number of the bank. He dialed. A husky female voice answered.

"Carla, it's Bo Tully. I need to talk to one of the FBI agents. Her name is Angela Phelps. She'll be the best looking agent there."

"The other agents are men," Carla said. "And one of them is pretty cute, Bo."

"Well, I'll have to check him out. But right now I need Agent Phelps."

While he waited for Agent Phelps, Tully swiveled around in his chair so he could look out the window at Lake Blight, but he couldn't actually see the lake because his window had been painted over. One of his local criminals had tried to shoot him from a boat bobbing about on the lake, an impossible shot, but he had missed Tully and Daisy by only about half an inch. The close-call had resulted in his unfortunate affair with Daisy.

Carla came back on. "Bo, Agent Phelps said she'll call you in a few minutes."

Tully thanked her and dialed the head janitor for the courthouse.

"Abe, get somebody up here to scrape the paint off my window. I've decided I prefer a view of the lake to the relative safety the paint provides."

"Okay, Sheriff, but we ain't painting it again."

"Tell me one more time, Abe, which of our corrupt county commissioners got you your job?"

"Harry Pulver. But he ain't as corrupt as Commissioner Phipps."

Tully smiled. "I guess you're right about that. I get confused over our commissioners' varying degrees of corruption. Which one had that county dirt road paved all the way out to his ranch in the mountains?"

"That's was Bob Lust. But he retired after he got the road paved."

"Right. I forgot. I guess the level of corruption must have taken a drop after Lust left."

"Clyde White replaced Lust."

"Ahh! That's why I didn't notice a decline. Anyway, Abe, I'd appreciate your getting the paint off the window sometime today."

"You got it, Bo."

Tully hung up, drummed his fingers on his desk and thought about calling Etta Gorsich. Being a psychic, Etta was probably already aware he was busy solving a bank robbery.

Somebody knocked on his door. Lurch stuck his head in. "You busy, boss?"

"Yeah, but come in anyway."

His phone rang. "Sheriff Bo Tully."

He motioned for the Unit to take a chair.

"Sheriff Bo Tully, this is FBI Agent Angela Phelps. I understand you had a call in for me."

"Angie! Great to hear you've been promoted!"

"Hey, it's still Blight City, Bo."

"True. But you weren't a SAC your last visit."

"Yeah, I made sure the FBI got most of the credit for solving the huckleberry murders. So what do you think about our bank robbery?"

Lurch handed him a slip of paper. Tully perused it: Vergil Thomas Stone, 27, 1204 W. Hemlock St., Blight City. Tully groaned. "Oh, I hate this job!" He looked up at Lurch and put his hand over the phone's mouthpiece. "I don't suppose you would go tell the widow Stone her husband is a suspect in a bank robbery, and, incidentally, was murdered today."

"Way over my pay grade, boss."

Tully turned back to the phone. "Angie, I've got a couple of things I need to take care of." He told her about the fingerprint on the tape and that Lurch had found a match. "I'll go out to visit the owner of the print first thing in the morning. This guy may be involved in the bank robbery someway. You want to come along and study my interrogation technique?"

"Are you kidding me, Bo? I wouldn't miss it for the world."

"Great! I'll I pick you up at your hotel at eight."

Tully shoved himself up from his chair and walked over to Daisy's desk. "I'm gone for the day, babe. Maybe for good."

"Why so glum, Bo?"

"I have to tell Mrs. Vergil Stone her husband is a bank robber, but she's now also a widow. You want to come along for moral support?"

"For her?"

"No, for me!"

"Not a chance!"

Tully rang the doorbell at 1204 W. Hemlock. The house was small and white with one scraggly tree alone in the middle of the yard, half a dozen brown leaves desperately clinging to it. A few neighboring lawns had toys scattered about, but this lawn was bare except for the tree and weeds. He hated reporting fatalities to the survivors, but at least this victim wasn't a teenager who had wrapped the family car around a utility pole. A pretty young woman opened the door, her thick blond hair tied back in a ponytail with a limp blue ribbon. Tully held up his badge. Her mouth gaped. "Oh no! Vergil's in trouble, isn't he?"

Tully identified himself and said, "Let's go inside, Mrs. Stone, and I'll tell you about it."

She led him into a small but comfortably furnished living room. Tully sat down in an easy chair and Mrs. Stone sat on a sofa across from him, leaning forward, her hands on her knees.

"Vergil's been arrested, hasn't he?"

"Well, no, I wish it were nothing more than that, Mrs. Stone. He's been murdered."

"Murdered!" She stared at him in disbelief, her mouth gaping.

Tully didn't know what to do. How do you handle this sort of thing? He thought maybe the department should hire someone who knew how to do it. The only way he knew was to blurt it out. Still, he thought he detected a sense of relief in Mrs. Stone. Perhaps murder was better than an arrest.

"What happened?" she asked.

"He was shot," Tully said.

"Shot! Why on earth would anyone want to shoot Vergil? Everybody liked Vergil!"

"He was shot from a considerable distance. It could have been a hunting accident, but I don't think so."

Mrs. Stone seemed to be sinking into the couch, growing smaller by the minute.

Tully asked, "Do you have children?"

She shook her head no. She was pretty but seemed tired, already worn down by something other than the murder of her husband. Tully put her age at about twenty-five.

"Do you work, Mrs. Stone?"

"I go to the community college. I'm in my second year of the nursing program, and I work weekends at Evergreen Assisted Living."

"How long have you and Vergil been married?"

She thought for moment. "Going on three years. We did all right for a while, until Vergil lost his job at the bank. He was the last hired and first fired when they had to cut back. He didn't like the job anyway. The manager said he would hire him again as soon as the economy picked up. Vergil hasn't had a job since he left the bank. I've been supporting us with my meager salary, but I have a well-to-do friend who's been paying my college tuition and books and even giving us some extra money. I had the feeling Vergil was going to do something stupid with some of those ratty friends of his. He was getting desperate. When he didn't come home the last few nights, I knew something was up."

Tully was still stuck on the fact Vergil had worked at the bank. "I hate to tell you this, Mrs. Stone, but I think Vergil was involved in a bank robbery."

Her eyes widened. "A bank robbery! Vergil? I can't believe it! Whatever faults he may have, Vergil is no bank robber. He doesn't have the nerves for it, Sheriff. He won't even set a mouse trap!"

Tully held up his hands. "At this point, Mrs. Stone, Vergil is only a suspect. Right now we have no proof he was in on the robbery. The money has yet to be found, but he was spotted on a mountainside near what appeared to be the getaway car. Did he own any guns, Mrs. Stone?"

"No! Vergil hates guns!"

"Some of his friends may hunt. They must have guns. Can you give me the names of his friends, Mrs Stone?"

"No, not really. Not the ones he's been hanging out with at a poolroom, staying out all hours of the night. I don't know where they live, but sometimes he doesn't bother to come home two or three nights in a row. Vergil mentioned them from time to time, but I can't recall any names. It's so strange. Vergil never had anything to do with that kind of people before."

"You're speaking of fairly recent friends?"

"Yes. I think they moved to the area in the past couple of weeks. I don't think they stay in Blight but in an abandoned cabin somewhere. Vergil told me he would like to see the cabin sometime because it sounded really interesting. Apparently it has a wonderful view, probably on the lake somewhere."

"Any other friends you can think of?

"Yes, old friends of his, but he doesn't have much to do with them anymore. When he did come home, I could tell he'd been drinking. He's been so upset about money I didn't bother him about that. I assume his friends paid for the drinks. You may wonder why I'm not more emotional about him being killed. I hate that he was murdered, but we were headed for a divorce, and I guess I'd already detached myself. Part of the problem, we had practically no money, but the big thing was, Vergil changed. It was like he was off somewhere with another life, maybe even another woman.

Everything was simply coming apart for us and had been for a long time."

Tully stood up. "I'm sorry to bring you bad news, Mrs. Stone. Do you have someone to stay with you tonight? If not, my secretary is a very nice person, and I'm sure she would be delighted to spend a few nights with you."

"Oh, I'll be all right, Sheriff. I have someone to stay with me, but thank you for offering your secretary."

Tully stood up to leave. "One last thing, Mrs. Stone. Do you have a picture of Vergil I can borrow?"

"A picture? I don't think so. We've never been much for pictures. Oh, we do have a wedding photo. I'll see if I can find it." She got up and walked into a hallway.

Tully had dozens of photos of his wife, Ginger, and many paintings of her. They always said that when they got old they would look back at the photos and laugh, but Ginger never had a chance to get old. He thought maybe he was just more sentimental than the Stones.

Mrs. Stone came down a hall from the back of the house and handed him a studio photograph. It had been cut in half, leaving only the husband. He studied it. Vergil Stone was the man killed on the mountain, all right. "I'll get the photo back to you, Mrs. Stone, as soon as I can."

"No hurry, Sheriff. I don't need it back."

Tully stopped at the door. "Mrs. Stone, what is your first name?"

"Danielle."

"By the way, Danielle, did Vergil own a black overcoat?"

"Why, yes, he does. It's the only warm coat he has."

Tully thanked her and walked back to his car. Danielle clearly wasn't one of those overly sentimental types.

Chapter 5

On the drive out to Gridley Shanks's place the next morning, Angie filled Tully in on the robbery investigation. "It was a professional job. The robber had perfect timing and knew exactly what he was doing."

Tully glanced at her. "I don't believe it."

"What don't you believe?"

"That our victim on the mountain knew what he was doing."

"Just listen to me for a minute. The manager typically shows up at the bank at a quarter to ten. The cashiers and other employees arrive at nine. The assistant manager shows up a little earlier than the tellers. The time lock on the safe goes off at nine-fifteen. The cash is counted out and distributed to the cashiers. When the manager arrives, he checks out the vault, and if he's satisfied, he closes it and the time lock resets. The vault can't be opened until after the bank closes for the day. All a robber can get is what's in the cash drawers."

Tully stopped at a stop sign before pulling onto Highway 95 and waited for a truck loaded down with Christmas trees to lumber by.

Angie thumbed through a notebook on her lap. "Yesterday morning a man stepped up to the manager just as he got to the bank door and stuck a gun in his ribs. They walked into the bank together. The manager did as he was told. The robber yelled for everybody else to lie down on the floor and shut their eyes. The vault was still open. Some of the employees peeked and saw the robber step into the vault and sweep blocks of cash off a counting table into a big black plastic trash bag until it was over half full. Then he slung the bag over his shoulder and walked out the door. Several employees jumped up and saw an old tan-colored car, probably a Datson, roar out of the parking lot. One of them got a partial plate number and called your office with a description. There were two people in the car. We don't know yet exactly how much cash he got, but it was a lot."

Tully turned south on Highway 95. "Sounds like the guy was a pro all right. On the other hand, I can't believe the guy at the bank was the guy killed on the mountain. You have any idea how tall the robber was?"

"The manager claims to be six feet tall himself," Angie said. "The robber was shorter. He estimated about five eight."

"How was he dressed?"

"A red-and-black checkered mackinaw, black pants, boots, a gray wool cap with an attached wool ski mask he pulled down over his face."

Tully glanced at her. "Definitely not our vic on the mountain. My guess is our vic was left in the car to keep it running. Sounds as if our robber in the bank had done this sort of thing before, doesn't it."

Angie nodded. "Yeah, it does."

Tully turned onto Culver Road, bounded on each side by small farms, the fields now covered with stubble and weeds. Some of the farms had long rows of Christmas trees in various stages of growth, some tall enough to cut and be hauled off to market. Maybe he should grow Christmas trees on his place. Might involve work though. When he was a kid, he and Pap would drive up into the mountains and chop their Christmas tree out of the national forest. Farmers back then would have thought you were crazy if you suggested they grow Christmas trees to sell.

Angie said, "So what do you think?"

"Christmas trees could be a lot of work."

"Are you listening to me at all?" she snapped. "I asked what do you think about how tall the robber was!"

"My robber? If the guy who robbed the bank was five foot eight, our vic couldn't be the robber. Vergil was almost six feet tall. I just don't think he could handle a robbery, anyway. The guy who did it sounds like a pro to me. Vergil no doubt was the guy left in the car to keep it running. Since he had worked in the bank, he probably gave the real robbers the inside information."

Angie stared out her side window. "Would you mind explaining something to me again, Bo?"

"Always glad to oblige a pretty lady. What do you want to know?"

"Explain the Blight way to me once again, would you?"

"Sure. Let me think a second." He scratched his jaw and frowned. "Well, the Blight way goes like this. It's pretty simple. Instead of going by all the pesky rules and regulations that govern a person's life, you simply do what feels right. As a law enforcement person, of course, I don't recommend the Blight way as a proper course of action."

"Yeah, right."

They came to a wooded area: jack pine, fir, and tamarack scattered sparsely about on each side of the highway. Tully slowed to check names on mailboxes. They passed one with "SHANKS" printed across the side in large black letters. He stopped, backed up and turned into a driveway that wound in and out among the trees.

Angie gasped. "Good gosh, Bo, this driveway is fantastic! It looks like the yellow-brick road in *The Wizard of Oz!*"

"Tamarack trees," Tully said. "This time of year they turn quite a few roads around here bright yellow with their needles. One of them turned our vic up on the mountain a bright yellow, too."

"Back East we call them larch."

"Larch is too wimpy for Idaho," Tully said. "Tamarack has a much more masculine sound. It's the classic firewood of Idaho. When I was a kid, we burned nothing but buckskin tamarack. There's one over there."

"Oh!" Angie cried.

"Yeah, it's a big old buckskin tamarack snag. Haven't seen one like it in years. "

"I'm not gasping over your stupid firewood, Bo! A woman just ran out of the house, got something out of a car, and ran back in."

"So?"

"She was stark naked! She wasn't wearing a stitch of clothes!"

"Whoa! And here I was looking at a stupid tamarack!"

"You missed something all right! She was gorgeous!"

"Now my day is ruined!"

The house was built of logs, probably taken from the property by the owner himself. Tully pulled up in front of it and turned off the engine. "Let's go knock on the door and hope the lady will answer it the same way. With my luck we'll get the wizard."

The door was made of thick slabs of wood and appeared more appropriate for a fort, as if someone might attempt to batter it down. Well, good luck with that. A lady opened the door. She was indeed gorgeous, even wearing a housecoat, which barely contained her voluptuous figure. He sensed she wore nothing under it.

"Oh no!" she gasped. "Sheriff Tully! I just ran out to get something out of the car and didn't notice you drive in."

"I missed you, too. I guess I was too busy admiring your buckskin tamarack. I assume you're Mrs. Shanks."

She seemed relieved. "Yes, I am. I suppose you're here to see my husband."

"We are. This lady is Angela Phelps. Miss Phelps is an agent with the FBI."

"The FBI! My goodness! Well, whatever it is, Grid didn't do it!"

Angie said, “He’s not a suspect, Mrs. Shanks. “We only came to ask him a few of questions.”

“He might be back soon. Maybe. I’m actually not sure. I never know about Grid. One time he had just planted a new lawn when a friend stopped by to invite him out for a beer. When he got back, the grass was six inches high. So I never really know when he might be back.”

“Sounds like my kind of guy,” Tully said.

Angie smiled. “So you’re telling us your husband doesn’t keep regular hours.”

Mrs. Shanks laughed. “Yes, I guess that’s what I’m telling you. Say, I was just about to sit down and have a cup of coffee. Would you all like some?”

Angie glanced at Tully. “I would love a cup.”

“Me too,” he said.

“Great!” Mrs. Shanks pointed to a kitchen table sturdy enough to hold a tank. “Grab a seat. I just made some banana bread. It’s still warm. Could I interest you in some?”

“Sounds wonderful,” Tully said.

Mrs. Shanks set three sturdy cups on the table and filled them from a massive coffee pot she took from a massive wood stove. Everything about the Shanks seemed massive.

Tully glanced into the living room. One whole wall was filled with books. On the wall opposite was a rack of rifles and shotguns.

He nodded at the books. “You must be quite the reader, Mrs. Shanks.”

“Oh, please, call me Sil. Well, actually I’m not a great reader, Sheriff. They’re all Grid’s. He’s very smart. He’s read every one of them. Every supper he lectures me about philosophy and history and literature, and I don't know what all. I tell you, Sheriff, if you want to be bored stiff you should come over for supper sometime."

"I may take you up on that, Sil. I'm kind of a book person myself. You mind if I take a look at Gridley's library?"

"Look all you want. You can even take some home with you, if you find something you like."

Tully walked over and checked the books. A lot of philosophy, science, and literature. He squatted down so he could see the bottom shelf. "Wow!" he said, glancing over at Sil. "What a collection of bird books! One of you must be quite the birder."

"Oh, my goodness, yes! Grid got into bird watching a few years ago and became fascinated with it. He had to drag me along on his outings to look for birds, and pretty soon I got interested in them myself. We've gone all over the country, working on our life lists. I think Grid knows every kind of bird in the whole country by sight. I get a little bored with it at times, but it gives us a wonderful excuse to travel. Are either of you a birder?"

Angie shook her head. "Not me, Sil. "Maybe someday, though."

"I kind of am," Tully said. "For the first time in my life I saw a mountain bluebird a few weeks ago, after looking for half my life. The mountain bluebird in Idaho almost got wiped out fifty or so years ago when some government agency sprayed its nesting area from a plane, but I think it must be coming back. Mostly now when it comes to birds I'm partial to fried grouse."

Sil laughed. "I'm with you there, Sheriff! But I'm afraid Grid has got me excited about birding. Maybe it's the travel. I'm one of those people who need an excuse to travel."

Angie finished her slice of banana bread and smiled. "Sil, that is the best banana bread I've ever eaten!"

"Why, thank you, Angie. We eat lots of it. Here's the strange thing. Whenever the bananas turn slightly brown, Riker's Grocery dumps them out back to be picked up by the garbage man. Grid swings by at five o'clock every Tuesday morning and picks up enough fruit and vegetables to last an army for a month. He drops most of it off for poor families he knows. Grid does the same thing with Helman's Bakery. They sell day-old bread for twenty-five cents a loaf. Any bread you buy from a store is almost a day old anyway, at least that's what Grid claims."

Angie, undeterred by learning the source of the bananas, munched a second slice appreciatively. "How many children do you have, Sil?"

"None, I'm sorry to say. Grid has two from another marriage, both of them smart as whips. They live with Grid's ex and her husband, both of them nice people. That's where Grid is right now. Little Grid just started first grade. He already knows how to read, but him and his teacher haven't been getting along. So Grid went over to the school to get everything straightened out."

Tully walked back to the table. He had just sat down and bitten into his second piece of banana bread when he heard a car pull up outside. He wasn't sure how Shanks would respond to a sheriff sitting at his table munching his wife's banana bread. The door burst open. If Genghis Khan had ever been recreated and stood well over six feet tall and been shaped like a steel splitting wedge, he might have looked a good deal like Gridley Shanks. Tully imagined little Grid at three feet tall but the same shape. The image made him smile. He stood up and stuck out his hand. "Mr. Shanks, I'm Sheriff Bo Tully."

Shanks shook his hand. "I know who you are, Sheriff. Everybody in Blight County knows Sheriff Tully. When I saw the sheriff's car out front, I figured I was in big trouble."

"Not at all. Oh, this lady gobbling down your wife's banana bread is FBI Agent Angela Phelps."

Angie stood up, smiled, and stuck out her hand.

"FBI! I must be moving up in the world." Shanks shook Angie's hand.

"How did it go at the school?" Sil asked.

"That first grade teacher is a mousy creature and didn't have a clue about handling little Grid. So I had a chat with the principal, and he moved the boy up to second grade, even though he's just turned six. That second-grade teacher has some steel in her, and she and little Grid hit it right off. I think I'm done with that problem. You got any children, Sheriff?"

"No, my wife died ten years ago, and I never remarried."

"Sorry. I knew that and forgot. So what brings you out here to the wilderness?"

Tully sat back down and took a sip of coffee. "A piece of flagging tape we found tied to a tree not too far from a murder victim."

"Oh, oh. What did the murder victim look like?"

"A young fellow. Vergil Stone by name. Lost his job a while back. We think he was involved in the bank robbery, but we can't be sure."

"What about the flagging tape brought you out here? There are strips of the stuff strung all over the county."

"This one had your fingerprint on it."

Sil sucked in her breath.

Shanks frowned and thought for a moment. "I've got pieces of property all over Blight County. But I don't mark them with flagging tape. Hey, this tape didn't happen to be hanging from a tree limb out on Canyon Crick Road, did it?"

"That's the one."

Shanks laughed. "That tape does mark some property I own. A couple fellows I met the other night asked if they could hunt elk there. I told them they could. I own about two hundred acres on the side of Chimney Rock Mountain. I put up the piece of tape to show these fellows the middle of my property, which reaches up to the crest. I told them to make sure they hunt that part of the mountain, because the owners on either side of mine get a little upset with trespassers. Anyway, there's a game trail up near the chimney. Elk use it sometimes, when they get run out of the canyon on the other side of the ridge. If these two fellows went over the ridge and dropped down into the canyon, they would be on Forest Service land. It's a hellhole down there and the elk love it. Just about anybody could shoot an elk there, but it would take a real hunter to pack it out. These two talked the talk of real hunters."

"You think they might have been hunting on the mountain yesterday morning?"

"That was the plan. I ran into them the other night over at Slade's. That's a bar on the north side."

"I know it well," Tully said.

"I bet you do, Sheriff. Anyway, we got to talking elk, and I told them a herd had been hanging around my property. They asked if they could hunt it. I don't have anything against elk, mind you, but I told them they could hunt there and that I would mark the middle of my land with flagging tape. And that's what I did."

Tully said, "If they were out there yesterday morning, they might have noticed something useful to us. We don't have much. Those two hunters, they hang out at Slade's on a regular basis?"

"Don't know. The other night was the first time I've seen them there. Only talked to them the once. They're not from around here, but I don't recall they mentioned where they did come from. They said they would see me back there tonight to let me know how the hunt went."

"Maybe you could meet me there and arrange an introduction, if the two of them show up again?"

"You buying, Sheriff?"

Tully laughed. "No, Grid, the county's buying."

"Excellent! I'll get the use of some of my tax money. I think they planned on hunting for the whole week."

Tully dug out his pocket notebook. "Can you give me their names?"

Shanks leaned back in his chair and peered up at the ceiling as if the names might be written there. "Oh boy, I'm terrible at names. Let's see, the big one was

Beeker and the shorter one, Dance. Horace Beeker and Ed Dance.

Tully helped himself to another piece of banana bread.

Gridley smiled. "I heard some talk today about the robbery, but it never occurred to me I might be involved. I try not to think too much about things that don't involve me."

"Sounds like a good idea," Tully said. "Seems as if just about anything that happens in Blight County involves me."

"That's what you get for being sheriff. Now me, I hang out mostly with lowlifes. Hear lots of chatter about what's going on in the criminal world. If ever I can be of any help, Bo, just let me know."

"Thanks. Any help you can give me will be much appreciated. By the way, Grid, I understand from Sil you two are quite the birders."

Shanks face lit up. "I can't tell you how much I hate that term 'birder,' but I guess I am one. I love it. We've traveled all over the country looking for the little rascals, and I've life-listed every one in the country except, I think, the ivory-billed woodpecker. It's supposed to be extinct, but a couple of fellows down in Arkansas claim to have seen one. One of these days we're going to head down to Arkansas, Sil and me, and see if we can find one. You a birder, Sheriff?"

"Sort of. I go through periods of enthusiasm and even have a life list."

"Any other hobby?"

"Yeah, I do, but I'm afraid it doesn't involve birds."

Shanks laughed. "Enough said."

Tully thanked Sil for the coffee and banana bread and stood up. "It's already getting pretty late. How about if I see you at Slade's about ten tonight, Grid?"

"You bet, Sheriff."

Angie got up and joined Tully at the door. She thanked Sil and shook Gridley's hand.

"By the way, Mr. Shanks," she said, "what do you do for a living?"

Gridley thought for a moment. "Not all that much, ma'am. I'm what folks around here call a hustler. I buy cheap and sell cheap and pick up everything free I can. But I don't steal, at least if there's any other way. I get old cars and fix them up with parts from other old cars. Make a little profit. Mostly, I try not to need money. An awful lot of life is wasted in the pursuit of money, and I try to avoid that. Someday, though, I'm taking Sil on a trip around the world."

Angie smiled at Sil and said, "I'm going to cruise around the world someday myself, Sil. Maybe we'll meet up out there."

Sil smiled back at her. "I hope so, Angie."

As they stepped outside Tully noticed that Grid had parked a bright red Cadillac sedan next to the Sheriff Department's battered Ford Explorer. It had been a long while since he had seen tail fins.

"I see you're admiring my Caddy," Grid said from behind them.

"Yes, indeed. Haven't seen one like it in thirty years."

"Yep, not many of them around anymore. I picked it up from a classic little old lady who got herself too old to drive. It wasn't in much better shape than she was, but I restored what wasn't. On the car that is. Less than ninety thousand miles on her—the car, not the old lady. Come to think of it, she's probably got at least that much on her too."

Tully smiled. "I bet gas was about twenty-five cents a gallon when the Caddy was new."

Shanks laughed. "You got that right, Sheriff. It now costs me five dollars in gas to get to the end of my driveway. I don't drive it much, except when I want to impress somebody, like a school principal."

"That work?"

"Like a charm. He thinks I must be rich to drive a car like this. Rich people can cause a school principal lots of grief."

"They cause sheriffs lots of grief too," Tully said.

Shanks smiled. "I expect so."

Tully glanced into an open-sided structure that Shanks apparently used for a woodshed. Parked near the rear between two neat stacks of firewood—buckskin tamarack, Tully was willing to bet—was a red four-wheel-drive all-terrain vehicle. He knew it was a four-wheel-drive because he had been drooling over ads for the exact same vehicle. "I see you do some off-roading, Grid."

"Actually, not all that much. I got that one at a great price. It's for sale. Everything I own is for sale. If you're interested, we could go out for a run sometime."

"I may take you up on that."

As they were driving out, Tully noticed scattered among the trees, several old vehicles including a pickup truck, and most in various stages of disrepair. What bothered him the most, the truck had two bales of hay in its bed. Then Angie pointed to a blue car door leaning up against a tree. "What do you suppose that's doing out here?"

Tully hit the brakes and backed up. He checked his rear- view mirror to see if Shanks had gone back inside. He had. "I think I'll take a look at this." He got out, walked around the Explorer, squatted down and looked at the door. A patch of rust the size of Tully's hand coated the door where the paint had been knocked off. In the middle of the rust was a hole the size of a dime. He ran a finger around the edge of the hole, then stood up and looked back at the doorway of the house. Shanks had opened the door and stood there watching him. "Exactly twenty-five yards, Bo!" he shouted. "Did it from this doorway with a .45 automatic!"

"That's pretty fair shooting, Grid!"

"Yeah, I thought so!"

"Mighty impressive!"

Shanks waved and went back in the house.

When Tully climbed back in the car, Angie said, "What's so impressive about hitting an old car door at twenty-five yards?"

"He hit the same hole three times."

"Three times! How could you tell that?"

"Because there are two little crescent shapes taken out of the sides of the hole, each about the size of a fingernail clipping."

As they turned back onto the highway, Tully glanced at the FBI agent. "Well, Angie, what did you think of Gridley Shanks?"

"To tell the truth, I was overwhelmed. I don't think I've ever met anyone quite like him."

Tully smiled. "He's probably an original, all right. Oh, maybe if you go back a couple hundred years, you might find the likes of him. What did you think of Sil?"

"She was absolutely gorgeous. I don't think she had a stitch on beneath that housecoat."

"Really? I can't say I noticed."

Angie laughed. "Yeah, right!"

"Well, I may have suspected, but that's not the sort of thing I ponder on."

"I'm sure. You think Grid had anything to do with the robbery and murder, Bo?"

"I don't like to think so, but I wouldn't rule him out. It's odd to find a single fingerprint, even a partial one like that, on a strip of flagging tape, unless the tape has been wiped. Then you have to ask yourself, why would anyone wipe a strip of flagging tape? Maybe I'll have a better idea after I talk to the two fellows he let hunt on his land. They may have been up there hunting at the time of the shooting and maybe they heard or saw something. You think Grid was involved in the robbery, Angie?"

"He's probably capable of just about anything. But I really liked him, Bo."

"Let me tell you something, Miss FBI. You will never meet a confidence man you don't like."

"You think he's a con man?"

"The best I've ever run into."

Chapter 6

Tully and Angie grabbed an early dinner at Crabbs. Lester Cline, the manager, seated them at their usual table. Tully dined with so many women he was amazed Lester could keep track of them all, matching each couple to a certain table. Maybe he had them all on computer: Bo and Susan: Table 8. Bo and Daisy: Table 12, Bo and Etta: Table 4, Bo and Angie: Table . . .

Angie said, "Why, Lester, this is the same table we ate at the last two times!"

"Yes, it is," Lester said. "I just thought it would be nice if you and Bo had a regular table, now you're back in town for a while. I keep certain tables open most nights depending on . . ."

Tully interrupted him. "That's very nice of you, Lester. Now how about some menus?"

"Coming up, Bo. I was just saying to the agent . . ."

"And a couple glasses of wine. What would you like, Angie?"

"I'll have Pinot Grigio."

"Make that two," Tully said.

"Good choice. And what kind of dressing with your salads?"

They both took blue cheese on the side. Lester went to get the wine, then stopped and returned to the table. "Oh, I forgot to ask. What kind of bread? The rolls are particularly nice."

Tully shook his head. "No matter how carefully you give your order, the waiter always has one more question. We'll both take the rolls, Lester."

"Good choice, Bo."

Angie said, "It must be nice to be known everywhere you go, Bo."

"Not that nice, actually. You may find this hard to believe, Angie, but there are people around the county who are not fond of me. I know that seems crazy, but it's true."

Lester brought their wine, left, and returned with the rolls and salads. Angie took a sip of her wine. She pursed her lips and blinked. "Where do you get your Pinot Grigio, Lester?"

"Would you believe we make it ourselves?"

"Yes, I would," Tully said.

"Well, actually we don't. We get it from a local winery that just started up. It's owned by a lady who gave up the cow business for the grape business."

Tully took a sip. "I have to say, it's interesting. You sure she gave up the cow business?"

"Pretty sure. Let me know if you get a sharp pain behind the eyes. There will still be a chance we can save you."

"Thanks a lot."

Lester went back to the kitchen.

Tully said, "You asked about my suspects. Right now Gridley Shanks is one of them."

"Suspected of what?"

"I don't know. Just a suspect. Maybe he's involved in the bank robbery. Maybe he's the shooter. We're not all that picky in Blight County law enforcement when it comes to suspects. I'm sure the murder is connected to the robbery. Maybe the flagging tape is too. Maybe it was the signal where our victim was to dump the getaway car and head up the mountain to make his escape. And to be shot."

"But if Shanks was involved, why would he offer to introduce you to the two hunters who might be involved too?"

"Because it would have been awkward not to. He had to have some reason for hanging up the flagging tape, and he couldn't think of a lie. So he went with the truth, kind of the truth anyway."

Lester returned to take their orders. Tully went with the garlic steak and Angie the wood-grilled shrimp.

"I'm surprised they have a wood grill at Crabbs," Angie said.

"They don't," Tully said. "They fake it. The grilled shrimp are still pretty good, though."

"So they cook the Blight way?"

"You're starting to catch on, Angie."

Tully dropped Angie off at her hotel. She said, "Please come in for a drink, Bo. They have a very nice bar."

"I would love to, but I may have to do some serious drinking later tonight."

"Ah yes, work, work, work." She laughed and gave him a peck on the cheek. Tully wiggled his toes to see if they had uncurled. There are pecks on the cheek and then there are pecks on the cheek. This was one of the latter.

Chapter 7

That evening Tully parked three blocks away from Slade's on the other side of the street. As he approached the entrance he could tell it was packed with a rowdy bunch, including the local motorcycle gang and numerous other Blight City characters. If he was ever to meet the person who murdered Vergil, he suspected it would be at Slade's.

The roar of the crowd diminished slightly when he walked through the bar's front door, but only for a brief moment. Then it picked up, the brave music of a local blue-grass band barely audible above the roar of the crowd. A big-bearded biker slapped Tully on the shoulder.

"What brings you to this dive, Bo? Out slumming?"

"Looking for bad guys, Mitch. Seen any around?"

The biker laughed and made a circular motion with his hand to indicate the entire crowd. "Take your pick."

Tully shoved his way through to the bar and found Grid sipping a beer, his hat resting on an empty stool next to him.

"I saved one for you, Bo!" Grid shouted above the roar. "A stool is pretty hard to find in here this time of night!" He lifted the hat and put it on. Tully sat down on the stool. Shanks jerked his thumb in the direction of two men seated next to him. He shouted above the roar: "Horace Beeker and Ed Dance!"

Beeker loomed over the smaller Dance. Both men reached around Shanks and gave him limp handshakes.

Tully turned to Shanks. "I know a bunch of the crowd in here, Grid, and they're pretty tough. I'm surprised one of them didn't just swat your hat off the stool and sit down!"

Grid shouted back, "Oh, that happened once before, when I was saving a seat for a friend of mine. Since then, nobody has bothered my hat a single time! Don't know why."

"Well, maybe Slade's is drawing a more civilized crowd these days. You think?"

"Could be. Hey there, bartender. Give my friend here a drink!"

The young bartender ignored him and continued talking to a couple of scruffy individuals across the bar.

"Service in here isn't what it used to be," Tully said. "It's always been awful, but it's worse now." He yelled at the young bartender. "Hey, bud, we need a little service here."

"Hold your horses!" the bartender snapped back. He went on chatting with his friends.

"Excuse me a second, Grid. Oh, you and your friends might want to lift your drinks off the bar for a few seconds."

Grid and the men next to him picked up their drinks and leaned back. Tully grabbed a hinged section of the bar, picked it up and slammed it over with a crash. The crowd went silent. Tully walked behind the bar, gave the bartender a hard shove, then stood there studying the bottles of liquor on a set of shelves. Picking up the most expensive bottle he could see, he grabbed four glasses, walked back, gave the hinged section a flip, banged it back into place, and sat down next to Grid. He filled the four glasses, then set the bottle on the bar in front of them.

Bit by bit the roar of the crowd resumed, although now with a great deal of laughter.

Grid said, "Remind me not to try your patience, Bo."

Tully smiled. "Ever so often, Grid, a person has to make a grand gesture when dealing with the likes of Slade's' clientele. Among other things, it helps keep our criminals in line and rudeness at a minimum."

Grid laughed. "It worked on me. I feel a whole lot politer myself."

Joey, the regular bartender, walked down behind the bar. "Sorry about that, Bo. The kid's new. I suspect he'll mind his manners in the future. Anyway, the bottle is on the house."

"Thanks, Joey, but we're doing work. I'll put it on the county card. Otherwise folks will think I'm taking graft."

Joey laughed. "If you don't take graft, Bo, folks will think you're putting on airs! Just ask Pap. It's on the house!"

"You win, Joey!"

Grid said. "You seem to be well known at Slade's, Bo! Who's Pap?"

"My father. He was sheriff of Blight county for many years and holds the record for corruption, womanizing, legal and illegal killings, and the same for gambling. The FBI got after him once, and he ran off to Mexico. Lived down there until the county cooled off enough for him to come back. Slade's is not my favorite hangout, but I do some of my best work here. Bad guys seem attracted to the place. No offense, Grid."

"None taken. Say, there's a little all-night cafe down the street. What say we move down there, where we can at least hear ourselves think?"

"Good idea! I'll get Joey paid for the bottle of whiskey and drinks and meet you outside."

"Suits me."

Joey put the bottle in a sack and handed it to Tully along with his county credit card. "Sorry about the rudeness, Bo. Any time you come in, your drinks are on the house from now on."

"Thanks, Joey. But I'm afraid that actually would be graft. We'll let the county pay." He walked out front and looked for Grid, Beeker, and Dance. They were leaning against the front wall of Slade's.

Beeker was tall and husky with a mop of reddish hair, more orange than red, to be exact. The other man, Dance, shorter and skinny with a thinning residue of light-brown hair. Tully had never before laid eyes on either of them. He said, "You fellows must be new in town."

"Yeah," Beeker said. "We came here a few days ago to hunt elk. Looked all over for a place to stay and finally found a little cabin outside of Famine."

"Yeah," Dance said. "About the only thing it comes with is a wood stove and a view."

Beeker frowned at him. "The price was right anyway. Nothing. Got a supply of firewood in it, so a least we can stay warm."

"You're lucky to find anything," Tully said. "Blight County gets pretty crowded during elk season."

Grid said, "Hey, it's freezing out here. What say we walk down to the cafe and finish our chat there?"

Tully was surprised the place was still open. The four of them walked in and sat down in a booth. Tully turned the water glasses upright and filled each half full of whiskey. A waiter with sleeves rolled up to the top of bulging biceps walked over and handed out menus. He nodded at the bottle of whiskey. "I'm afraid that's against the law, fellows."

Tully smiled at him. "I'm the law in Blight county, son. We'll also have a round of coffee."

"Yes, sir," the waiter said and went to get the coffee.

Beeker was holding his glass of whiskey up off the table. "I just wanted to make sure you weren't going to make another grand gesture, Sheriff."

Tully laughed. "Don't worry, Horace. I limit myself to one a day."

The waiter came back with the coffee. "We serve breakfast anytime. You fellas want some?"

"Sounds great," Tully said. "I'll take hash browns, scrambled eggs, toast, and bacon, the bacon crisp."

The waiter looked around the table and got nods from the others.

"The same for all four. What kind of toast—white, whole grain, sourdough, or rye?"

Tully shook his head. No matter how thoroughly you think you've given your order, waiters always have one more question. "White," he said. The other three nodded in agreement.

The waiter left, returned with four mugs and poured their coffees from a large black thermos, which he left on the table.

Tully said to Beeker and Dance, "I'm sorry to take you fellows away from the pleasures of Slade's, but I'm investigating a murder out on the mountain where you were hunting this morning. You must have left your rifles and hunting outfits in your cabin. Not a good idea if the cabin's anywhere near Famine."

Beeker said, "Actually it's quite a ways outside of Famine. There's a spring nearby where we get drinking water, but it's starting to ice up. We leave all our gear in the cabin. It's remote enough, nobody should just be passing by."

"Remote is right," Dance said. "We might shoot an elk right from our front porch. Grid told us you want to know if we saw anything when we were out on his place yesterday, right Sheriff?"

"Yeah, I need all the info I can get, Ed. Anything you can remember would be great."

Dance said, "It was plenty cold, I can tell you that. We got there just before all the ruckus started, sirens all over the place. Heard a shot, but figured it was another hunter."

Tully sipped his coffee. "You have any luck?"

"Naw," Beeker said. "Not with all that ruckus. I did see a herd of deer come over the top of the ridge right up by that rock knob. It looked for a while like they might wander right down toward us. When they heard the shot, they scampered off, and we never saw them again."

Tully thought for a moment. "You remember what time you heard the shot?"

Dance looked at Beeker.

"Must have been close to ten," Beeker said. "I didn't check my watch."

"That's about right." Tully said. "What did you fellows do then?"

"A whole lot of people started showing up, so we got out of there," Beeker said.

"What kind of vehicle were you driving?"

"A pickup. An old Ford but it runs fine."

"Where did you park it?"

Beeker thought about this for a moment. "Grid had put a piece of orange flagging tape on a tree at the middle of his property and told us there was a wide spot to pull off fifty yards or so farther on. That's where we parked, but when the ruckus started we walked down to the truck and drove back to Famine."

"You see anything unusual?"

"Naw. Just that herd of deer, if that's unusual."

"You have scopes on your rifles?" Tully asked.

"Oh, sure," Beeker said. "That's how I spotted the deer. I was scoping the ridge when the herd came over the top."

"Where was that again?"

Beeker thought for a moment. "Right up next to that knob."

Gridley looked at his watch. "Oh, no! I'm late. I've got somebody I have to meet. You fellows help the sheriff out with anything he wants to know, but I have to run."

Tully said, "Thanks for the help, Grid. It is getting late. But we've got our breakfasts coming. I guess we'll have to share yours."

"Sounds good to me," Dance said.

"Me too," Beeker added. "I'm starving. You're sure this is on the county, Sheriff?"

"Indeed it is, Horace. It's the county's pleasure. If there's one thing Blight County loves, it's hunters. Everyone here hunts. I'm even a bit of a hunter myself. Every fall I fill my freezer up with venison. In recent years, it's been mostly filled up by the generosity of my deputies. I give them time off to hunt. How long have you fellows been hunting elk?"

"Years and years," Beeker said. "Ever since we was kids."

"Mostly big game?"

"Oh, yeah," Dance said. "We love hunting big game."

Tully thought the cafe's hash browns and scrambled eggs were about the best he'd ever eaten. When they had cleaned all four plates, Dance said, "I guess we better head back to our cabin. Be four in the morning before we get there, so I guess we'll sleep in. Thanks much for the whisky and breakfast, Sheriff. I didn't realize how hungry I was."

"Don't thank me," Tully said. "It's on the county." He glanced at his wristwatch. Eleven o'clock. "You fellas going to stick around for a while? With this cold weather blowing in, the elk hunting will pick up."

"Oh, yeah, we'll stick around," Dance said. "We have a week, maybe more"

They walked outside.

"Hope you get an elk," Tully said. He thought it was highly unlikely, though. If hunters can't tell a herd of deer from a herd of elk, their chances aren't that good. He stopped suddenly. "Oh, oh," he said. "I have to go back. I forgot to leave a tip for the waiter. The poor devil probably needs it, too."

"See you around, Sheriff," Beeker said. They went off down the street.

Tully walked back into the cafe. The waiter was clearing off their table and putting the dishes into a blue plastic dishpan. "Just leave the dishpan and everything else right where it is," he told the waiter. The man straightened and stared at him. Tully took out his badge and showed it to him. Then he took out his pocket notebook and opened it to two blank pages. "Press the fingers of your left hand on the left page and the fingers of your right hand onto the right page."

The waiter did as he was told.

"How'd you guess I done time, Sheriff? The tattoos?"

"Naw. Would you take a crappy job like this if you hadn't?"

"Good point. Just for your information, Sheriff, I've been clean ever since I got out."

"Don't worry about it. Now sign your name on the bottom of each page with your prints. I just want to distinguish them from those of my friends."

"You're some kind of friend, Sheriff."

"Aren't I though?" He pulled a roll of cash out of a pants pocket and thumbed through it until he found five twenties. He gave them to the waiter. The man almost fainted.

Tully stepped to the door and looked down the street. Beeker and Dance were nowhere in sight. "Listen to me now," he told the waiter. "I want you to leave the dishpan, dishes, and silverware right where they are. I'll drive up out front in a few minutes and come in and get them. You make up your own mind if you want to share your tip with the owner as rental for his dishpan and contents."

"Yeah, right."

"That's what I thought."

Tully walked the four blocks down the street to where he had parked his Explorer. Pugh leaned against it.

"You get the license plate on my friends' vehicle?"

Pugh handed him a slip of paper. "Right here, boss. I drove along after them for about a mile, until they took the Old River Road to Famine."

Tully studied the information. "So they're driving a late model Land Rover. Pretty ritzy. Oregon, huh?"

"Yeah."

"Trailer hitch?"

"No. I think it's mostly their town car. It's all polished up. I doubt it's ever been off pavement. The River Road will be a new experience for it. Maybe they want to avoid driving through Famine. You know, there's plenty of good elk hunting in Oregon. Funny they'd drive all the way to Blight County for elk."

"Be interesting to see if they bought out-of-state licenses to hunt in Idaho. Must have cost them a fortune. If they're driving a new Land Rover, I guess at least one of them can afford it. Oh, one more thing, Brian."

"Right, boss, I'll check with Fish and Game tomorrow to see what kind of licenses they bought, if any, and what addresses they used."

Tully smiled. "You're always one step ahead of me, Pugh. By the way, the names I got are Horace Beeker and Ed Dance."

Driving out to his house, Tully did a lot of thinking about Dance and Beeker. He didn't want them leaving the county without his knowing it. Hunters who can't tell elk from deer are always worth keeping an eye on. Suddenly, he hit the brakes and made a U-turn on the highway. It had just occurred to him there was something else he had intended to check.

He drove back to town and cruised quietly past 1204 West Hemlock. The house was dark. He drove to the end of the block and came back through the alley. A small garage sat off to one side of the alley behind the Stone's house. The rear end of a bright red car protruded far enough out that the garage doors couldn't close. It was only the second time in recent years Tully had seen tail fins.

The plot thickens, he thought. Grid lets two guys hunt his property who saw deer instead of elk. The flagging tape marking the place where the getaway car turned into the ditch has Grid's fingerprint on it. Now Grid is spending the night with the widow of the man shot on the mountain, a man suspected of being a bank robber. The shooter makes his escape on an ATV on the other side of the ridge. Grid has an ATV. He has a rack full of guns in his house and is an excellent shot. He has a pickup parked out in his woods with two bales of hay in it. The pickup parked on the road after the robbery had two bales of hay in it. Everything about this robbery had been arranged by someone very crafty. Grid is as crafty a man as he's ever met. He would have to take closer look at him. He wouldn't even mind taking a closer look at his wife.

Chapter 8

It was almost three when he started down the dirt road that sloped across the meadow to his log house. He and his wife, Ginger, had built the house themselves with logs from trees they had cut off their own land. The land had been a gift from a corrupt and violent old man, but enough about his father. Tully still appreciated his generosity. Building the house with Ginger had been the best time of his life. Ginger hadn't remembered it that way, but women tended to be so prissy when it came to wrestling logs.

Halfway across the meadow he braked to a stop and peered at the house. The living-room light was on. It hadn't been on when he left that morning. At least he couldn't believe he had left the light on. He turned off the Explorer's headlights, coasted down to the front of the house, and stopped. He unsnapped the retaining strap that held his Colt Commander in his shoulder holster and pulled the gun out. He opened the car door, got out, and pressed the door shut. Walking on the tips of his boots across the porch, he ever so carefully turned the knob on the front door with his left hand, the Colt Commander pointing straight up in his right, his finger on the trigger. He stepped in.

Daisy was asleep on the couch, a blanket spread over her. His watchdog, Clarence, was asleep on a pillow next to her, his head resting on her hip.

Tully tiptoed over to his bedroom, undressed, put on sweat shirt and sweat pants, and went to bed. He wasn't worried about burglars breaking in. His former watchdog was back. He had no idea how or why Clarence had suddenly returned. He had given him to a friend months ago. Well, not exactly a friend, but a person willing to accept Clarence. He guessed that anybody willing to accept Clarence had to be regarded as a friend. And now the miserable little beast was back.

Tully awoke to the racket of a large spoon beating on a metal pan.

"It's almost seven o'clock!" Daisy yelled. "Time a hard-working sheriff should be out of bed!"

Tully groaned, got up, and wandered out to the kitchen in his mismatched sweatshirt and sweatpants. Breakfast was on the table. Huckleberry pancakes and sausage links! He supposed Daisy wasn't a totally evil person. He pulled out a chair and sat down.

She laughed. "You look like something Clarence dragged in."

"If you're referring to my watchdog, Daisy, that's pretty bad. What's Clarence doing back? I thought I was rid of him for good. For that matter, what brings you out here?"

"What do you suppose, Bo? I was lonely and needed some company. All I found was Clarence sitting in a car with a dreadful old man."

Tully frowned and shook his head. "Batim Scragg! Daisy, he is so much worse than a dreadful old man. He is possibly the deadliest human being on the planet, if I exclude my father. Did Batim say why he was returning Clarence? I liked to think of them as two peas in a pod."

"He said Clarence kept chomping his chickens."

Clarence had climbed up on a chair at the end of the table and was staring at Tully, a questioning look in his eyes.

Tully stared back at him. "Oh, it's all right, Clarence. You can stay. But Daisy owes me big time."

Clarence's tail began to wag.

Daisy said, "I should think huckleberry pancakes would make us even for my rescuing your cute little dog."

"Not by a long shot, sweetheart. A down payment does occur to me, however."

Tully and Daisy's affair had ended months earlier, but neither of them had quite gotten over it. He got up, walked over, and gave her a quick smooch. "That's for the huckleberry pancakes. By the way, where did you find the huckleberries?"

"Your stash in the cellar. I used the ones from the freezer, but I noticed you canned some too. You're quite the handy guy, you know that, Bo? You'd make somebody a good wife."

"Thanks. I'll have to think about that. Actually, it was Rose who canned the huckleberries."

"Old as you are, you still have your momma looking after you."

"Yeah, and for a nosy old broad she does pretty well by me in the way of food."

Tully sat back down and sampled a pancake. "Hey, not bad, Daisy. You'd make somebody a pretty good wife yourself."

Daisy laughed. "Yeah, right! You had your chance, Bo, and you blew it."

"I thought you were the one who blew it?"

"No, it was you."

"Well, in that case, I'm sorry. By the way, I do have some gossip, if you're interested."

"I'm alway interested in gossip, Bo! Wait till I get a refill."

She grabbed the coffee pot off the stove and refilled both their cups. She replaced the coffee pot on the stove, sat back down at the table and folded her hands. "Now tell me! I love gossip."

Tully told her about seeing Grid's car parked in the widow Danielle Stone's garage.

Daisy responded, appropriately, with a gasped expletive.

Tully said, "Yeah, my word exactly. This adds a whole new dimension to the bank robbery and murder. I wouldn't be surprised if Grid ended up with both the widow and the loot from the bank."

"It's pretty cold blooded, Bo. You think Gridley Shanks is that cold blooded?"

"I think Grid can be any way he wants to be. The nasty part of this, he has a beautiful wife, absolutely gorgeous, and two young kids that live with a former wife and her husband. The shooting took place on a piece of land he owns. So he knows the terrain out there. He has two so-called hunters on his property who can't tell a herd of deer from a herd of elk. How they figure in, I don't know. I thought I heard an ATV take off on the other side of the ridge after the shooting. I saw a four-wheel-drive ATV at Grid's place. Suppose he has an affair going with Danielle Stone, Vergil's wife. He not only masterminds a robbery and somehow ends up back at her house with the loot, he does away with his competition for Danielle, her desperate husband. How does that sound?"

Daisy shook her head. "Pretty gruesome. You think this Grid is some kind of homicidal maniac?"

"I have to admit he doesn't seem like one. Maybe the secret to being a successful homicidal maniac is not to seem like one."

Daisy laughed. "Well, yeah, you go around acting like a homicidal maniac you're not going to last very long."

"My point exactly," Tully said.

"Maybe he's one of those weirdos who love to play dice with the devil. It gives him a rush and makes him feel smarter than everybody else."

Tully finished a huckleberry pancake and forked another onto his plate. "Good point. Maybe he figures I'll take his accomplices down, and he'll have the loot all to himself. I'll go check with the FBI guys and see if they've turned up anything."

"Angie?"

"No way. Notice I said guys."

He drove to the bank and parked at the edge of the shopping center's lot. Angie was nowhere to be seen, but two other agents were talking to the bank manager outside the front door. The manager pointed to something out in the parking lot. Tully looked but saw only empty blacktop. Maybe that's where the getaway car had been parked. The FBI could worry about the car and the robbery, he would worry about the man killed on the mountainside. Maybe Vergil was one of the robbers and maybe he wasn't. Maybe the car in the ditch wasn't the getaway car at all but only a car that looked like it. On the other hand, why was Vergil climbing the mountain if he wasn't trying to get away from the getaway car? And if he was the robber, where was the loot? And why was he shot? No doubt to silence him about others involved in the heist. And to take his share of the loot. It all made his head spin.

He walked over to the bank. The manager, Phil Estes, introduced him to the two agents. They shook hands.

"So you're the famous Sheriff Bo Tully of Blight County, Idaho," the one named Mel Jaspers said. "I expected you to be at least nine feet tall."

"Usually I am," Tully said, "but I've been feeling a little short the past few days. You fellas got the bank robbery solved yet?"

Shaun Dugan, white-haired and obviously the older of the two agents, shook his head. "It appears the robbers had some inside information. They pulled the thing off with perfect timing."

Tully tugged on the corner of his mustache and thought for a moment. Then he said, "The chap gunned down up on Chimney Mountain worked for the bank until a while back. He may be the one who helped with the timing. So far, though, we haven't found a penny of the loot."

"Good heavens!" the manager said. "You mean Vergil Stone! I can't believe Vergil was involved, but it appears he was."

Jaspers said, "There's a lot of loot to find. Shaun and I could retire and live in luxury on a Caribbean island, if we'd had the good sense to think of it. Apparently, the robbers made off with a bundle, actually a large garbage bag over half full."

The bank manager said, "Yeah, they made a big haul. It'll take us several days to figure out exactly how much."

Tully said, "Wow, if I'd known you had that much cash lying around, Phil . . ."

"Yeah, I know what you mean, Bo. We've never had a robbery before and didn't think much about having one. The reason we had so much cash on hand, loggers like it for pay day. A week later the robbers would have got some, all right, but not the big haul they did."

Jaspers said, "It's pretty obvious they had inside information."

"Yeah," Tully said. "You need inside information for a haul like that. Makes a person think about taking up bank robbery as a sideline."

"It's a pretty crowded field right now," Jaspers said. "With the economy down like it is, I doubt you'd find any openings, Bo."

Tully shook his head. "Just my luck. Alway a day late and a dollar short."

He told the agents he would see them later and then drove over to the courthouse and parked in the spot reserved for the sheriff. His three-thousand-dollar alligator-skin boots klocked nicely as he went up the stairs. A man who knows his boots notices such things. Boots were the only thing Tully splurged on. Anyone wearing boots that expensive instantly drew respect in Blight County. He had paid for them with money from the sale of one of his watercolors. That was the most he had ever been paid for one of his paintings and he knew, finally, that he could now make a living from his art, modest though it might be. The boots had earned him the respect of the county commissioners, even though they knew he hadn't paid for them with graft. They may have been ignorant of the art world, but they understood graft. The holder of a public office never buys anything that showy and expensive with graft. It would set off alarms all over the place. Commissioners go around with holes in their jackets and the soles flopping on their old shoes. But as all the residents of Blight County knew most of their local politicians were corrupt. But they could be bought cheap. Even a poor person could own at least one. As long as the politicians kept themselves affordable, Blight citizens put up with them. The system worked, and nearly everybody was satisfied. It was the Blight way.

When he got to the briefing room, all the deputies were out on patrol. Only Daisy, Lurch, Herb, and Florence were there, Herb reading his newspaper as usual, Daisy on the phone.

"Why thank you, dear," she said sweetly. "We always try to be of service in situations like this. You're very welcome, dear."

She hung up the phone and shouted at Tully. "You volunteered me to do what! Sit all night with the grieving widow of a man who has just been murdered! Are you out of your mind, Bo?" She had inserted a popular expletive randomly throughout the diatribe.

Tully shrugged and walked over to Lurch's corner. "Find any info on Vergil Stone?"

"Yeah, but nothing you don't already know."

Tully went into his office. Daisy followed him in.

She pointed to his window. "I hope you like the view. One of the janitors about drove us crazy scrapping the paint off. The screeching was awful. I still get shivers up my spine."

"Your screeching probably got on his nerves, too." Tully spun around in his chair and looked at the lake. For as much as the window paint had irritated him, he hadn't even noticed it was gone. He swung back around and pointed to a chair. Daisy sat. "One of your jobs from now on, Daisy, will be to watch for any boat out on the lake with a man in it holding a rifle."

"Sure, Bo, no problem. I was just hoping you would come up with an extra chore for me when I wasn't sitting with the widows of murder victims."

"Yeah, yeah," he said. "You have such a hard job. So maybe you can tell me the name of the weather girl at the TV station?"

"Don't you ever watch the weather on TV, boss?"

"Once in a while, but the weather girl is so cute I don't hear what she's saying."

"Her name is Wendy Crooks."

"See if you can get her on the phone for me."

Daisy frowned at him. "I can't believe you want to talk to a weather girl!"

"I need her to help me solve a murder."

Daisy laughed. "You really are desperate, Bo." She went back to her desk and a few minutes later yelled at him. "Wendy on line one, boss!"

Tully picked up. "Wendy, I need you to help me solve a murder. Is there anyway you can check your Doppler thing and tell me the exact time we got a brief snow flurry out on Chimney Rock Mountain, say between six and ten Monday morning?"

"Yeah, we'll still have it, Sheriff. I'll see what I can find and get back to you. If we don't have it here at the station, I'll have it at home. I record all my weather casts so I can evaluate my performance later. I just get better and better, Sheriff."

"That certainly has been my impression, Wendy."

"Thanks, Sheriff. I'll get back to you as soon as I find out. That's Chimney Rock Mountain between six and ten a.m. Monday, right?"

"You got it, Wendy." He hung up.

Lurch stuck his head in the door. "I got five sets of prints off that mess in the blue dishpan. One set is yours, one is Shank's, and three others belong to guys who have all done time for robbery."

"Great! I thought so!" He took out his pocket notebook and opened it to the pages the waiter had pressed his finger prints on. He handed the open notebook to the Unit. "You can eliminate this guy. He's the waiter. The other two sets belong to two of our bank robbers, if my guess is correct."

"Great, boss!"

"I'm pleased you appreciate my effort, Lurch. Anything going on here besides our murder and bank robbery?"

"Not much. Oh, one of the deputies arrested Petey again."

"Petey! I can't believe it! What this time?"

"Another chain saw."

"A chain saw! Petey doesn't even know how to run a chain saw! Why does he keep stealing them?"

Lurch shook his head. "I don't know. I guess because they're not nailed down. Maybe he figures he can sell it to someone. Luther Hawkins called up and said somebody stole a chain saw out of his garage. Petey lives a couple blocks away. The deputies picked up Hawkins, drove over to Petey's house and found the chain saw on his back porch. So they hauled Petey to jail."

Tully sighed. "I wish they would stop doing that. I'd better go down and talk to him. Petey's probably starting to think of jail as his home away from home."

Lulu, the jail matron, was sitting at her desk when Tully walked in.

"Come to see the vermin, Bo?"

"One in particular. Petey!"

"Oh, dear. When Petey's out for more than a week, I start to worry about him."

"Yeah, well, I worry about him, too, Lulu. Don't they have special places for people like Petey?"

"Yeah, they do. They call it jail. If it's not tied down, Petey takes it home with him. I guess this time he walked into a garage and made off with a chain saw. That's getting pretty close to burglary, Bo. Old Judge Patterson might even send him away."

"Patterson is senile enough, he might do just that!"

"Don't knock old Patterson, Bo. He gives you just about anything you ask for."

"Yes, he does, but I don't want to risk sending Petey up before him again. Go bring the criminal out here, Lulu."

"You going to resort to the Blight way again, Sheriff?"

"Afraid so. Destroy all the paperwork you have, and go up and make sure Daisy takes care of any in the office. I'll have a word with the deputies and Luther Hawkins."

Lulu shook her head. "Hawkins will be tough."

"I'll handle Hawkins."

As Tully drove Petey back to his house, he warned the little man, "You steal one more thing, Petey, I'm not saving you. This is the last time."

"But, Bo, it was only a chain saw. I couldn't even get it started. Luther probably couldn't start it either. You shouldn't arrest a person for taking a piece of junk."

"Petey, if the piece of junk is in a person's garage, it's his personal junk. You take it, you're stealing. Given your record, you could go to jail for a long, long time. Maybe even to prison. For a stupid chain saw that doesn't even run! One more time before Judge Patterson, and you could be on your way."

"Luther Hawkins is gonna be pretty mad at you, Bo, for letting me go."

"I'll take care of Hawkins. You take care of Petey."

"I still don't think I should have been arrested."

Tully rolled his eyes. "This is the last time I bail you out, Petey, and I mean it. I don't care how many times I've done it before, this is the last!"

Tully drove up in front of Petey's house, shoved the criminal out the door and watched the little man walk up the driveway muttering to himself.

Tully made a U-turn in the street and drove down to Luther Hawkins's house. He parked, walked up, and beat on the door. Hawkins answered.

"Luther, I just let Petey out of jail, and I don't want you raising a fuss about it."

"Bo, this is the second time he's stolen my chain saw!"

"I don't care. The chain saw doesn't run anyway."

"I know. That doesn't mean I shouldn't report it getting stolen."

"Listen to me very carefully, Luther. You perhaps remember the shop-lifting charge I made go away."

"But that was all a mistake! I completely forgot about that package of pork chops!"

"You had it stuck down the front of your pants, Luther. Nobody forgets what's stuck down the front of his pants. Ed Riker is still mad at me for getting you off."

"I appreciate it, Sheriff. I'd appreciate it a lot more if I'd got to keep the pork chops. My mouth still waters when I think about them."

Tully sighed. He hadn't felt like eating a pork chop since arresting Luther. "I'm sorry about your pork chops, and I'm sorry about the theft of your broken chain saw, and I've put them ahead of several other things like a murder and a bank robbery, but now I have to get back to solving those minor crimes."

"Oh, all right, Bo. As a favor to you, I'll forget Petey stole my chain saw."

"Good. I appreciate it."

Back at the courthouse, Tully went up to his office and flopped into his chair. Then he got up and walked to the door. "Hey, Lurch!" he yelled across the briefing room. "Come in here for a second."

Lurch sauntered over and took a chair across the desk from Tully. "Yeah, boss?"

"You turn up anything of interest on our victim?

"Got the bullet analyzed. It's a seven-millimeter, all right. If you find the rifle that fired it, we can get a match."

"Seven millimeter. That's an elk-hunting caliber. Could be a hunting accident."

"Possible, but I don't think so," Lurch said. "I couldn't find a shell casing, so the shooter must have picked it up. In a hunting situation, it seems likely he would have jettisoned the empty and jacked a fresh shell into the chamber. My guess is he worried about the empty. Maybe he's done this sort of thing before."

"Maybe he likes being tidy."

"He also had a scope on the rifle."

"How do you know that?"

"I measured the distance between the grove of trees and the body. A hundred and twenty yards. That would be a heck of a shot with open sights, nailing a guy precisely between the shoulder blades. The guy knew something about shooting. At least a scope would have let him see clearly that his target was a man. You don't snap off a shot at something over a hundred yards. He would have had to rest the rifle on something, maybe a tree limb. I just don't think you would risk an off-hand shot at that distance."

"It wasn't a tree limb he rested the rifle on, Lurch, it was his knees. He shot from a sitting position. Dave Perkins found two little scuff marks where the shooter dug in his heels. No criticism of your good work."

"Dave Perkins? Dave is as good as it gets."

"There's one more thing, though."

"What's that?"

"Dave showed me an impression the shooter made with his rear end. I'd like you to make a cast of it."

"A cast of a rear end! I've never made a cast of a rear-end. Supposing I do get a usable cast, whose rear end are we going to compare it to?"

"Maybe the shooter's, if we ever find him."

Lurch scratched his head and frowned. "Do you think rear ends are unique to each individual, Bo?"

"I don't know. I've seen some unique ones, though."

"Let's leave Daisy's out of this, Bo." Lurch burst out laughing at his own joke. Tully joined in.

Daisy popped open the door. "What's so funny? I know it has to be nasty."

All Tully and Lurch could do was shake their heads. "Forget about that impression," he told Lurch.

Daisy's phone rang, and she went to get it. She picked up and said "Sheriff's Department." She listened and then said, "One moment please." She covered the mouth piece and yelled. "Your weather girl on line one, boss!"

Tully walked back to his office, slid into his chair, and picked up. "Yes, Wendy."

She said, " I hope this will help you solve your murder, Sheriff."

"I hope so too, Wendy. What did you find?"

"That dusting of snow on Chimney Rock Mountain was very brief. It started at 6:00 in the morning and ended at 6:30."

"Super! Thanks, Wendy, you've been a big help. I'll let you know how this turns out. Maybe I'll take you to lunch as a token of my appreciation."

"That would be wonderful, Sheriff!"

He thanked her again and hung up.

Daisy was standing in his doorway. "Lunch wouldn't be your only token of appreciation."

"This is serious, Daisy. It could unlock our whole mystery."

Daisy walked back to her desk shaking her head.

He studied the time for the snow flurry. Very interesting. Here he had thought Beeker was the type who couldn't tell a herd of deer from a herd of elk. To get a dusting of snow in their tracks, the deer would have had to go through between six and six-thirty, which means Beeker would have had to be on the mountain then. He had actually seen the herd of deer, which meant he had to be on the mountain nearly four hours before he claimed to be, over three hours before Tully and the deputies showed up on the scene. What would he have been doing there that early, except getting prepared for Vergil before anyone else showed up?

That afternoon Tully drove over to Judge Patterson's house. Mrs. Patterson answered the door. "Why, Bo! How nice to see you! You need to drop by more often."

"Why, thank you, Mildred." He whispered to her. "Does the judge still drink single-malt?"

She whispered back. "Yes, but he's awfully stingy with it. You'd think he paid for it himself."

"One of the perks of being a judge, Mildred."

"I suppose. There should be some perks."

"Is himself available?"

"Yes, dear. Unfortunately. Otherwise you and I could have a little party, you know what I mean?" She winked at him.

"I do, indeed, Mildred. The thought of such a party keeps me awake nights."

"Ha! You lie, Bo. But I like it. I'd better go get his holiness, before we get carried away. Grab a chair in the living room. He's locked up in his study, supposedly going over some points of law."

Tully doubted old Patterson had even stumbled over a point of law in thirty years.

The old man came harrumphing into the living room, closely pursued by his wife.

"So, Bo, you managed to track me down in my lair on one of my few days off."

"Sorry about that, Judge. It's just that criminal investigation waits for no man, and I'm not sure how much time I have to get to the bottom of this one. So I need a search warrant pronto."

"Good heavens! You don't expect me to have search warrant forms here at home, do you?"

"That's my expectation. If you don't have a real one, I figure you could phony up something that looks like one. I have to serve it today. So it would be nice if you put yesterday's date on it."

"Bo, the things you ask me to do for you, we could both be thrown in prison!"

"It's the Blight way, Judge."

"The Blight way! I get so sick and tired of that phrase. Well, it so happens I do have some search-warrant blanks in my study. Give me the pertinent info you need on it."

Tully thanked the judge and gave him the information.

"Gridley Shanks?" Patterson said. "That's a new one on me. I thought all of our citizens had passed through our legal system by now."

"Really, Judge, I'm surprised this Shanks fellow hasn't come to your attention before."

"He probably has. I vaguely remember the name. A name like that is hard to forget."

Mildred said, "While you're writing that up, Judge, Bo and I will have a drink!"

"Good idea, my dear. I think we have some rather decent bourbon left, enough for the three of us."

"Actually, I think Bo might prefer some of the single-malt."

"Oh, by all means. I'd forgotten all about the single-malt."

Mildred winked at Bo. "I'll be right back. You take anything with your scotch, Bo?"

"A glass would be perfect, Mildred."

She returned shortly with a tray of drinks, all of them substantial.

Tully sipped his. Perfect. He thought it was too bad he hadn't gone to law school and become a judge. At moments like this, that boring grind seemed almost worth it.

Mildred sat down on a couch, a coffee table between her and Tully. She sat very straight and proper and took tiny sips of her scotch. "I have to tell you, Bo, I was very upset when I heard you and Daisy had broken up."

"Yeah," Tully said. "I was pretty upset myself. Actually, I was kind of surprised so many people knew we had a thing going. We tried to keep it a secret. How did you hear about it?"

"Oh, I really shouldn't say."

"It was Rose, wasn't it?"

"Your own mother! Good heavens, no!"

"Remember, Mildred, wives of judges are not allowed to lie."

"I didn't know that. You're right, of course. Your mother let it slip one day while we were having lunch."

He and Mildred had barely finished their scotch when Judge Patterson walked in. "I don't know why I let you draw me into your various schemes, Bo, but here's your doctored-up warrant for a seven-millimeter rifle from one Gridley Shanks."

"Thanks, Judge. Just remember it's all in the cause of proper law enforcement for the citizens of Blight County."

"If you say so. I think it smacks an awful lot of the Blight way."

"Well, that too. But I'm sure you'll agree, Judge, that we have to fall back on what works, not stick to minor legalities."

The next morning Tully drove over to the Shanks'. The red Cadillac was nowhere to be seen. He parked in front of the open-sided woodshed, again glancing at the four-wheel-drive all-terrain vehicle parked near the back. He knew it was four- wheel-drive because he himself had longed for that particular model. If Shanks had one, he thought the only decent thing was for the county to buy its sheriff one. He imagined a chase with him on one ATV and Grid on the another.

He knocked on the door. Sil answered. He was disappointed to see she was fully dressed.

"Why, Bo, what brings you out here?"

"Sorry to bother you, Sil, but I need to see Grid."

"You may have to wait awhile. I haven't seen him for a couple of days."

"Do you have any idea where he might be?"

Sil laughed. "None at all, Sheriff. I learned long ago not to waste my time trying to keep track of Grid. He could be in Japan for all I know."

Tully glanced at the rack of rifles and shotguns on the wall across from the bookshelves. There had to be twenty or more firearms there, ranging from black-powder firearms to modern rifles to shotguns to handguns, all showing signs of serious use. He heard a car pull up outside.

Sil said, "You're in luck, Sheriff. There's Grid now."

Tully wasn't at all sure about the luck part.

Shanks came through the door. "Back already, Bo?"

"Yeah, Grid, but I'm afraid my visit doesn't give me any great pleasure, though." Tully handed him the warrant. He detected no sign of annoyance as the man read it. Shanks then walked across the room and with one powerful sweep of his arm sent all the rifles and shotguns clattering to the floor.

"I think there's a seven-millimeter or two in there somewhere, Sheriff. Help yourself."

Tully said, "I'm not impressed with grand gesture, Grid, but that's as good a one as I ever seen."

Grid's eyes widened in surprise. Then he smiled. "Usually I get at least a shocked reaction with that one," he said. "Anyway, you might find a seven-millimeter rifle in that mess."

Tully studied the mess. "I suppose," he said. "I'd much rather take a look at where you keep the good stuff."

Tully glanced at Sil. She hadn't reacted. She had seen it all before. He looked back at Shanks. The man showed no signs of rage, anger, or even annoyance. "So tell me, where do you keep the good ones, Grid?"

Shanks stared silently at him for a moment and then laughed. "In the bedroom. I do have a seven-millimeter in there. I suppose you want to take it."

"Correct. Since there's no point in owning two seven- millimeters, I assume you have only one in the bedroom. Nevertheless I should check for myself."

Shanks showed Tully into the bedroom. As he expected, the double bed was neatly made and beautifully covered with a patchwork quilt. The room was in perfect order. Tully studied the rifles carefully. "Well, I'll be darned. You have two seven- millimeter rifles in here, Grid. I'm afraid I'll have to pencil in a two on the search warrant, if you don't mind."

Grid said, "You can do that?"

"Search warrants can change. Hey, what's this? A forty- five automatic and a revolver."

Grid frowned. "I suppose you're going to pencil them in on your search warrant."

"Naw, that wouldn't be legal, Grid. I'll have Judge Patterson add them to my list later."

"Yeah, go ahead and take them. I haven't killed more than half a dozen men with those pieces."

Tully smiled. "I doubt that, Grid, but I will take them, with your permission. Just put your signature next to my note about taking your forty-five and the revolver, to show I had your permission." Shanks shook his head as if in disbelief, but then signed his name.

"Now, if you don't mind," Tully said, "I'd like to have a little chat with you out in my car." He put a handgun under each arm and carried the two rifles out to the Explorer. "Mind opening the hatch door, Grid?"

Shanks opened the door. Tully put the guns in the cargo area.

Shanks said, "You want me in the front seat or the back, Bo?"

"Front seat will be fine, at least for now. I want to run a theory by you."

They got in the car. Tully started it and turned up the heater. He reminded Shanks about how he had given permission for two men to hunt his property, men he had just met. The flagging tape with Shanks's partial print had been right where the getaway car was parked. One of the hunters had shown up there four hours before he claimed to be there. In other words, something very strange was going on with Gridley Shanks.

The suspect showed not the slightest reaction to Tully's theory. "You done?" Shanks asked.

"That's basically the picture, Grid. It's why you keep showing up on my radar"

"No offense, Bo, but you and I are both the victims of converging incidentals."

"Converging incidentals?"

"Yes. Let's start with the flagging tape. I have no idea how only a partial fingerprint of mind ended up on the tape. Except for that, you would never have gotten me involved. Then there are the two so-called hunters, Dance and Beeker, which are the reason I put up the tape in the first place. I wasn't aware Dance and Beeker didn't know the slightest thing about hunting, only that they were looking for a place to hunt. I had just met them. They both talked elk like old pros. They knew the language and . . ."

Tully interrupted. "I suspected they knew nothing about hunting when Beeker seemed to mistake a herd of elk for a herd of deer. Turned out he did see a herd of deer, because the deer came through during the snow shower, which lasted between six and six-thirty. He didn't see the herd of elk, because by the time they came through, he had stationed himself in the woods, waiting for Vergil to show up."

"Could be," Shanks said. "You think Beeker shot Vergil?"

"Yes, I do. One other thing, Grid, the other night I drove down the alley behind Danielle Stone's house and saw the tail fins of a bright red Cadillac sticking out of her garage."

A flash of anger crossed Grid's face. He sat in silence for several seconds. "Okay, you got me there. I didn't expect you to go snooping around in the middle of the night, so I didn't tell you everything. I can explain it, but I don't want Sil to know about this. Danielle is my daughter. Vergil was such a fool, I didn't even like talking to him. I'd been giving Danielle money all along. As a matter of fact, I own their house and let them live there for free. I don't know if Vergil knew about the money I gave Danielle, but that's how they survived. I also paid for Danielle's tuition at the community college, along with her books. Vergil was such a wimp! I couldn't believe he had enough guts to get involved in a bank robbery. It was a step up for him. He worked for the bank a while back, but got laid off. Since then he worked a couple of nothing jobs. But when I heard

Vergil had been killed, I couldn't believe it. He wasn't a bad guy, just a wimp."

Tully said, "Suppose you had set up the robbery, Grid. How would you have done it?"

"Probably just the way it was done."

"And how was that?"

"I've given some thought to it, from what I've read in the paper. First, I'd find a desperate loser like Vergil, one who knew the bank routine but was mad at the bank for laying him off. Then I'd talk him into robbing the bank, because he had worked there and knew the schedules and timing and everything. I never expected Vergil actually to get involved in a bank robbery. He would turn to jelly right in the middle of it, maybe even before. I'm sure he was used only to supply inside information. The other robbers would know he was a weak link. The cops would break him in seconds. The only safe thing to do was use him as a decoy and take him out after the robbery. Plus they could divide up his share of the loot."

Tully tugged the droopy corner of his mustache. "So Vergil gives Beeker and Dance the inside information, and they use him as a decoy, the driver of the getaway car." He sighed. "Only one guy robbed the bank. Which one do you think?"

"The little I know about them, I'd say Dance."

"Where's Beeker?"

"I don't know. You seem to think he was on the mountain waiting to shoot Vergil. I'm guessing everything, Bo. I doubt Vergil would even have thought of running out on Beeker and Dance."

Shanks thought for a moment. "Vergil probably was desperate enough to go along with the robbery, as long as he didn't actually have to hold a gun on anybody. I don't think they had to worry about him taking off. Someone like Vergil wouldn't have the nerve to run out on guys like Dance and Beeker."

"Now for the big question, Grid. Where's the loot?"

Shanks shook his head. "I don't have a clue. I can tell you this, if I was in on a bank robbery, I'd keep an eye on the loot no matter what. I wouldn't let it out of my sight. You're taking a big risk, robbing a bank. You have to be aware your associates are crooks, and that any one of them will take off with the whole caboodle if given half a chance."

Tully said, "You think Vergil was the kind of person to take part in a robbery?"

Shanks thought a moment. "He was desperate. Desperate people do desperate things. But to tell you the truth, Bo, I can't imagine Vergil holding a gun on anybody."

Tully said, "So you think Vergil was just the driver."

"Must have been."

"So what happened to the guy that robbed the bank?" Tully asked. "Say Dance was the robber. What's Beeker doing?"

Shanks thought for a moment. "Maybe it's like you said. He's the one who shot Vergil. Maybe that's why he arrived at the mountain early enough to see the deer."

Tully tapped his fingers up and down on the steering wheel. After a moment he said, "Or maybe there's a fourth guy, in addition to Beeker, Dance, and Vergil. Maybe he's the shooter."

"A fourth guy? Could be. I've never seen anyone else with Beeker and Dance, though."

Tully had. One Gridley Shanks. A person who owned an ATV, and who was also an excellent shot.

Shanks said, "I tell you, Bo, you got all these converging circumstances pointing at me, and that's all they are, irrelevant lines of suspicion. You haven't found a single fact tying me to the robbery or murder, and that's because there isn't any to find."

Tully shook his head. "I'm sorry, Grid. You're right, I don't have a single fact tying you to the murder or robbery. And it would make me extremely unhappy if I did. It's just that every time I pick up a fact, it seems to point to you."

"That's all right, Bo. I know you're just doing your job. No hard feelings. But do me a favor. Don't ever mention Danielle to Sil. If a wife finds out you've been even slightly involved with another woman, it kills something inside of her. The rest of her life she has this little dead spot in there, and the dead spot's got your initials on it. Sil and I were young and just married when that stupid affair happened. I don't have many secrets from Sil, but that's one I'd like to keep."

"Sil won't find out about Danielle from me, Grid. I'll have Lurch return the guns as soon as he's checked them out."

Chapter 9

Tully went back to the office and dropped Shanks's rifles and handguns off for Lurch to check their bullets against the one that killed Vergil. Then he drove over to the bank. The FBI agents were packing up to leave and head to the airport. Angie was seated in the bank manager's office. She was writing something in her notebook when Tully walked in. She smiled, stood up, shook hands with the manager. Tully exchanged pleasantries with Estes and then walked outside with Angie.

He asked, "You think Estes is involved in the robbery?"

"Always a possibility, but I don't think so."

"Any leads?"

Angie shook her head. "No, we're wrapping things up here. The lone robber shoved a gun in the manager's ribs when he arrived for work. Forced him to unlock the door. The manager is about six feet tall and he says the robber was a bit shorter, maybe five eight. He had an accomplice waiting for him in the getaway car, but no one saw him clearly enough to get a description. Several employees saw the car and described it to police, and the police broadcast the description of the car on police radio. I guess that's where you came in, Bo."

"Yeah, we were practically on top of the car, but I'm afraid about all we have are some casts of tracks and a wild theory or two. We haven't turned up one dollar of the loot. Your massive resources help you find out anything on a Horace Beeker or Edward Dance?

"Both of them have done time for robbery."

Tully nodded. "That's what my CSI Unit tells me. Oddly, Fish and Game probably has license information on them. It could be phony, but probably not. Maybe they were here to hunt elk. It would be risky to try that with phony licenses. If they were stopped by a game warden, the whole plan could fall apart. Even pretending to hunt, they needed licenses. Or maybe they simply would have shot any game warden who checked them. He would have been a minor nuisance. These could be really bad guys, but I interviewed both of them the night after the killing of Vergil Stone, and if one of them murdered him they are pretty cold customers."

Tully gave her the spelling of the names and the vehicle license number. She wrote them down in her notebook. She said, "Any idea where these two characters might be now?"

"Not much. One of them said something about a cabin somewhere around Famine."

"Famine? That's where Dave lives."

"Yeah, it's a little town about thirty miles west of here. I have some contacts over there besides Dave and will try to find out if anyone knows any Beekers or Dances in the area."

Angie wrote furiously in her notebook. "Remember this is an FBI case, Bo."

"The FBI can have the bank robbery," he said. "The murder is mine. There's no proof yet the victim was connected to the robbery, except he appeared to be fleeing in a vehicle matching the description of the getaway car."

She gave him a hard look. "I hope the Blight way isn't kicking in here."

"The Blight way?" he said. "What's that?"

"You know darn good and well what it is. It's the Blight County system of law enforcement that's a little weak on the law part."

"There you go again, hurting my feelings, Angie."

"I hope so. Just for once, Bo, I'd like you to play by the rules."

"I always play by the rules."

"Yeah, your rules."

"My rules or not, Angie, right now our suspects could be halfway to Portland, Seattle, or San Francisco. And those are only our suspects. Hard to tell where the guys are who actually robbed the bank."

He walked Angie out to her rental car. "I think it's pretty clear right now that we know who the driver of the getaway car was. It was a young fellow by the name of Vergil Stone. He was employed by the bank up until a few months ago and gave the two heavies the routine at the bank. That's how the robber timed his entrance to the vault's still being open."

Angie shook her head. "How do you find out all this stuff anyway?"

"Crime detection."

"And the Blight way?"

"That too. By the way, how much did these guys score?"

"The manager thinks a huge amount. They'll have a more accurate figure tomorrow."

Tully tugged on his mustache. "Any chance you can get away from the robbery for a day. I have a tiny lead taking us over to Famine tomorrow. You're welcome to come along. The guys we're after could be the bank robbers. If not, they might do in a pinch."

Angie shook her head and smiled, her hand on the handle of the car door. "Hmm. I'll see what the other agents say. Are you by any chance meeting up with Dave?"

"Perkins? Yeah. As a matter of fact we are, because I may need a tracker. You interested in our fake Indian?"

"What makes you think that?"

"Just your basic detection. I seem to recall you spent quite a bit of time with him your last case over here."

Angie smiled, got in her car and drove off. Tully drove to the office. The troops appeared hard at work. They must have heard the heels of his boots klocking down the marble-chip floor of the courthouse. He walked over to Lurch's corner. The Unit was tapping madly away on his computer.

Tully stood there until Lurch looked up.

"Geez, boss! You scared me!"

"I was just wondering if, between computer games, you have time to check out the bullet that murdered young Vergil Stone against the seven-millimeter rifles and handguns I have stashed in my car." He handed the Unit the keys to his Explorer.

"I'll get on them this minute, boss. You turn up any possible leads?"

"No. I have a couple of fragile clues. I want you to use that computer of yours for something other than games to see if you can find a record of any Beekers or Dances living in Blight County. I doubt if any of them had anything to do with robbing the bank, but they may have some idea who pulled it off."

Tully walked back toward his office and stopped at Daisy's desk, bending over to whisper in her ear. "What do you have planned for my breakfast tomorrow?"

"Don't you wish," she said. "I'm afraid you'll be back to your Egg McMuffin for tomorrow, Sheriff, because I happen to have a date tonight. I do have a life, you know."

"A date? With whom, may I ask?"

"Not that it's any of your business, but Clyde Fisk invited me to dinner at Crabbs."

"Fisk! He walks into a crowded room, he lowers the average IQ by twenty points!"

"This is Blight City, Bo. A girl takes what's available. And believe me, what's available is a pretty sorry mess. No offense."

"None taken. Listen, sweetheart, you're coming down with a bad case of the flu. Fisk will understand. Get over it about the time I get back from Famine."

"Is that a proposal?"

"Close as I can come at the moment. What do you say?"

Daisy thought for a moment. Then she put her hand over her mouth and pretended to cough.

Tully smiled. He went into his office and slid into his chair. After spinning around and contemplating Lake Blight for a few moments, he punched a number into his phone.

A female voice answered. "Dave's House of Fry. How may I help you?"

"The boss around, Mavis? Tell him Sheriff Tully wants to speak to him."

"One second, Bo. He's in the kitchen. I'll go fetch him."

Fetch. Not often you hear that word anymore. Maybe old words survive only in tiny isolated places like Famine.

Mavis came back on. "Dave will be here in a sec. I haven't seen you over this way in a while, Bo."

"You miss me, Mavis?"

"Sure. But not all that much."

"You still hanging out with that vacuous boyfriend of yours?"

"Roy isn't all that vacuous anymore, Bo."

"How vacuous is he?"

"I don't know. I think Doc Millbank gave him some pills for that. They just haven't kicked in yet, as far as I can tell."

"He ever find work, Mavis?"

"Sometimes. The pickings over here in Famine are pretty thin, Bo. At least Roy works some of the time. Right now he's pulling off the green chain at the mill."

"The green chain! Marry him right away, Mavis. Men drop dead pulling off the green chain."

"And your point is?"

"Insurance, Mavis, insurance. You can't be dumb."

"Next time you're over, Sheriff, we'll have to discuss this a little more. Here's Dave."

Dave came on. "You trying to pick up my best waitress, Bo? First your old man runs off with my most beautiful waitress, and now the son is zeroing in on Mavis. A man can hardly stay in business with the Tullys around."

"Don't get excited, Dave. I have more women problems at the moment than I can shake a stick at. I just can't help flirting with them. It's in my nature."

"Must be nice, having more women than you can shake a stick at."

"Not bad at all. As you know, I'm dealing with the inconveniences of a bank robbery and a murder over here in Blight City. What I'm calling about, have you ever heard of any folks over there by the names of Dance or Beeker?"

"Dance? Nope, can't say I have."

"How about Beeker?"

"Beeker. That rings a bell. It's an old name around here, but I don't know of any Beekers still living here. You know Batim Scragg. Batim's lived here practically forever. He might know of some Beekers past or present."

"Good idea. Thanks, Dave. By the way, I may need your services tomorrow."

"Anything interesting?

"Maybe. Might involve some shooting." He clicked off.

Pugh walked in and grabbed a chair across from Tully. As was his practice, he spun the chair around, sat down astraddle of it, and propped his arms on the back.

Tully leaned back in his chair. "What do you know about the little town of Famine, Brian?"

"Famine?" Pugh thought for a moment. "I know that fifty percent of the population aspires to ignorance."

"What about the other fifty percent?"

"They've attained it."

Tully smiled. "I'm headed over there tomorrow. Probably be gone a few days. You'll be in charge."

"What about Daisy?"

"When you're away, she'll be in charge. But you take care of any major stuff that happens. You should be able to reach me on my phone at any time, but don't use the radio."

Pugh stared off in the distance.

"What are you thinking, Brian?"

"Nothing. I see you got the paint scraped off your window."

Tully frowned. "Maybe I should let Daisy handle the major stuff, too."

"Naw, I can do it, boss. You going after Beeker and Dance?"

"That's my plan. If things get sticky, I may need you and Ernie. So be ready to drop everything and move fast. I don't have any idea how bad these guys are."

"You going alone?"

Tully checked the doorway to make sure Daisy wasn't listening. "No, I'm taking Angie."

Pugh smiled. "I'd take her too, but that's not a lot of firepower. How about Pap?"

Tully frowned. "Just once I'd like to handle one of these situations without dragging my old man in. On the other hand, he would never forgive me if I left him out, particularly if some killing is involved."

"You think there will be killing?"

"Somebody took out Vergil Stone, and if it was Dance or Beeker, neither one of them was much bothered by it. It was cold-blooded, premeditated killing. If they're the ones, I don't think they would hesitate to take one or all of us out, particularly if they're looking at a long prison term."

"Fish and Game didn't have any record of licenses for them." Pugh said. Tully rocked back in his chair and laced his fingers together behind his head "They must not have been concerned about being stopped by a game warden while they were out pretending to be hunters."

Tully nodded. "Lurch found out they had both done time for robbery. Fish and Game would have checked that and refused to issue them licenses. So if these guys are as bad as I think they are, they would have popped any game warden who checked them for licenses."

Pugh said, "I suspect so."

Tully stood up, walked over to the door and yelled at the Unit. "Lurch! Come here!"

The Unit wandered over. "I'm pretty busy, boss, but what do you need?"

"Go over to the library and see if you can turn up anything with the name of Beeker or Dance on it."

He looked around the briefing room and saw his useless undersheriff, apparently about to make an exit. "Herb, stop! I've got a job for you, too. Check the county tax office, and see if you can find any Beekers or Dances listed there. Then go through all the newspapers at the library for the past month, and see if you can find any classified ads with ATVs for sale."

"Geez, boss, I'm loaded down with work already. I'll get on this first thing tomorrow."

Tully sighed. "No, Herb, right now. I need this info like an hour ago. So hop to it. Give the info to Daisy."

Herb went off, muttering. Pugh followed him, smiling.

Tully picked up his phone and dialed. Gridley Shanks answered.

"Hi, Grid. It's Bo Tully. I need some information. What do you know about Beeker and Dance?"

"Just what I've told you. Not all that much. They seemed nice enough fellows. Paid for drinks."

Tully turned his chair around so he could look at the lake. "I'm headed to Famine tomorrow to check out some things. You ever hear Beeker or Dance mention any relatives living in the area?"

"I don't recall any names. On the other hand, it's pretty hard to recall anything after a night at Slade's."

"One of them mentioned they were staying in a cabin somewhere outside of Famine. I thought it might belong to a relative of some kind."

"Could be, Bo. Sounds like something to check out. I don't know much about either Dance or Beeker. I'd help you out, if I could."

"Thanks anyway, Grid."

Tully punched in Angie's number.

"Hi."

"Hey, Bo! What's up?"

"You want to ride over to Famine with me tomorrow? I suspect our bank robbers may have stayed over there someplace. Maybe we can pick up some leads."

"Sounds good. We've done just about everything we can here at the bank. The last two two agents are headed back to the main office. I'm staying on at the hotel for a few days, in case we get some new leads. You want to pick me up at the hotel?"

"Yeah. Eight o'clock."

"I'll be waiting."

"Good. You might want to come armed."

"I always come armed when I'm out with you, Bo." She hung up.

Tully turned and looked up. Daisy was standing in the doorway, her hands on her hips. "And what is Daisy to do with the information Herb gives her?"

"Daisy is going to call on all the ads and see if the person who placed the ad sold the ATV. If the person gives you a hard time, I will personally go over, kick down his door, and get the info myself!"

"Okay, okay, don't get your tail in a knot, Sheriff."

Daisy went back to her desk. Tully shook his head. He had to create an atmosphere of more respect and discipline in the office. This, of course, would require avoiding any future affairs with his secretary. He got up and yelled across the briefing room. "Lurch, get in here!"

"You better hurry, Lurch," Daisy said. "Bo's in one of his moods."

"Great!" Lurch said, walking by Daisy's desk. "You get him in one of his moods, and I'm the one who suffers."

"Yeah," Tully said. "A lot of suffering you have to put up with, Lurch." He shut the door behind the Unit.

Lurch sat down in the chair across the desk. Tully had walked over to the window and was staring out at Lake Blight. He thought he could make out a rim of ice forming around the shoreline. Maybe this year the lake would freeze over enough to provide some decent ice fishing. He turned and frowned at the Unit. “I’m heading over to Famine tomorrow, and I’m leaving you in charge.”

“You’ve got to be kidding, boss!”

“I am. Actually, Daisy’s in charge, as usual. But I want you to do everything you can to pull this bank robbery and murder together. Whatever you need, get it. Follow up on everything you can think of. Try to find out where Dance and Beeker are staying. I think they’re holed up somewhere in the county, probably over around Famine, waiting for the heat from the bank robbery to die down before heading back to wherever they came from, Oregon apparently.”

“When will you be back?”

“Probably late tomorrow night and . . .”

A phone in the briefing room rang. Daisy answered it. “One moment please,” she said sweetly. Then she covered the mouth piece and yelled, “Hey, Bo, it’s your fortune-teller!”

Tully glared at her and picked up the phone.

“Hello?”

“Hi, Bo! It’s Etta.”

“Etta! Great to hear from you!”

“I really need to see you. It’s serious, Bo. Can you stop by for tea?”

Tully glanced at his watch. “Sure. How about in an hour?”

“That would be perfect. I don’t want to be a bother, Bo, but this is serious.”

“I hate serious, Etta. See you in a bit.” He hung up. Daisy was standing in the doorway. “I like a man who leaps at commands.” She smiled grimly.

"It's not what you think, Daisy. Etta is an attractive woman, all right, but she's ten years older than I am. We're not having an affair."

"Good, because I've been thinking of getting back together with you."

Lurch looked from one to the other.

Tully smiled. "Are you thinking our little mistake wasn't really a mistake?"

"That's what I've been thinking." she said. "I've even thought we should maybe get married."

Tully stared at her. "Making a mistake is one thing, Daisy. Getting crazy is another."

Daisy laughed. "I have one requirement, however. We keep Clarence."

Tully shook his head. "You don't take long to throw in a deal-breaker, do you? I'm planning to haul Clarence back to Batim Scragg tomorrow."

"Bo, I love that little dog, and he loves me. And only one of us chews the feathers off chickens."

Tully laughed. He was thinking of saying 'which one,' but decided not to push it. There were other ways to get rid of Clarence. He knew he loved Daisy. He also knew he probably would never again marry for love. He loved too many women. Ginger's death had crushed him. If he ever got married again, it would be to an amiable companion who could easily be replaced. His affair with Daisy had ended months before, and he still wasn't over her. Given time, the pain should subside, and he would be careful not to make the same mistake again.

The Unit seemed slightly dazed. "I hate it, boss, when I get caught in a row between two lovers."

"Forget everything you heard, Lurch. Now here's what I want you to do. There's a little old lady who works for the library. Her name is Vera. I want you to go over there and ask her to track down anything involving the name Beeker or Dance in Blight County. She's something of an expert on the history of the county. I think she's even written a book about Blight County. Okay?"

Lurch appeared dazed. "I'm still stuck on you and Daisy getting married."

Chapter 10

Etta's house was perched on a steep, weedy hill with a long set of rickety stairs leading up to it. If Etta had actually been a fortune-teller, the house would fit the occupation perfectly. Apparently, it was possible to drive around the hill and approach the back of the house by means of a road, but so far he had chosen to climb the stairs as if they were some kind of challenge he set for himself. Or perhaps the stairs were preparation for seeing Etta. The stairs had a handrail on each side, but Tully thought handrails were for sissies. He went up the stairs two steps at a time, his boots making loud, satisfying thumps. Tully was about to push the buzzer when the door suddenly sprang open. He jumped back, his right hand slipping under his vest.

"Bo!" Etta exclaimed. She stood on her tiptoes and gave him a peck on the cheek. "I was hoping that was you. Come in, come in. Grab a seat on the sofa, and I'll pour the tea."

Tully sat down in a chair across the coffee table from the couch.

"Great, Etta! I can use a good strong cup of your tea. I have to get back to the office and prepare some things for tomorrow."

Etta disappeared into the kitchen and soon returned with her silver tray, the silver teapot, silver sugar bowl, and cream pitcher. The china cups were so dainty Tully was almost afraid to touch one. His finger wouldn't fit through the handle so he grabbed the cup itself, ignoring the heat.

Etta sat down on the couch. "Bo, the reason I asked you over is that I wanted your company, but I'm also very worried about you."

"Worried about me, Etta? You don't have to be worried about me. You know I can take care of myself. Any risky situations, I send in one of my deputies."

"I know that isn't true. I may not be a fortune-teller, but I can always tell when you're lying."

Tully dumped two spoonfuls of sugar into his tea, stirred it and took a sip. Etta appeared seriously worried. He knew she wasn't a fortune-teller, but he had been startled numerous times by her pronouncements, things she knew about him that he was certain she had no reasonable way of knowing.

Etta peered at him over her tea cup as she took a sip. "You look tired, Bo. I hope you're taking care of yourself."

"Etta, I've given up just about everything I like to do. I haven't smoked my favorite pipe in five years. I keep it in a box out in the garage along with all my other pipes and smoking paraphernalia. I can't bear to throw any of it away. Every time I walk by the pipes cry out, 'Smoke me! Bo, smoke me!' It's very sad. So far, though, I haven't given in."

Etta laughed. "I hope you haven't given up on wine. You know wine is supposed to be good for you."

"Even the wine they serve at Crabbs? If I gave up eating at Crabbs altogether, I'd probably improve my health a hundred percent. So you wanted to warn me about something, Etta? I didn't think it was about my health."

"It wasn't your health, Bo, but something dreadful. I know you don't believe in my nonsense, but I sense a dark force hovering near you, and you appear totally oblivious to it. I just know you're in terrible danger and seem totally unaware of it."

He stared at her. "Danger is part of the job, Etta. You know that. I deal with bad guys all the time. It's something you get used to. There are people who would dearly love to kill me, I know that. Fortunately, most of them are in prison. That's one of the reasons they would like to kill me."

Etta frowned. "I know, dear. And I wish I could tell you the source of this new danger, but I can't. It's something out there that never quite takes shape. It's like a threatening dark force that hovers near you. It seems to be closing in on you."

Tully felt the hairs on the back of his neck twitch. A shiver went through him. She had piqued his interest. "Etta, you have any clues about what this dark force might be?"

"No! Nothing! It could be a person. And I feel terrible that I don't know what or who it is. I probably shouldn't have said anything, but I couldn't help myself. It's just this terribly vague sense of something very bad." She started to cry.

Tully got up, walked around the coffee table and sat down beside her. He reached his arm around her shoulders and gave her a hug. She gave a little cry. "Oh!"

"Etta, don't cry. Believe me, everything will turn out okay."

"Oh, it's not that, Bo. Your gun just jabbed me."

They both laughed

"Anyway, Etta, thanks for telling me. I'll be extra cautious from now on."

"Oh, I do hope so, dear. It's just that I sense this dark force converging on you. I know you must think I'm the weirdest person you've ever come across, but you mean a lot to me."

Etta wasn't the weirdest person Tully knew, but she was a contender. Still, he knew he could fall in love with her, and he already loved way too many women.

He stood up to go. *Converging!* Gridley Shanks leaped to mind. Sometimes there's a good reason all signs converge on a particular individual—he's guilty!

Back at the office, Tully tilted back in his chair, closed his eyes and laced his fingers together behind his neck. One of these days he would get out of the sheriffing business and just paint. His agent, Jean Runyan, had sold his latest painting for $2500. Not bad. It would be wonderful to wake up in the morning and not have to worry about bank robberies, murders, stolen chain saws, and convergences. Instead he would simply walk up to his studio sipping a hot cup of coffee and go to work on his next painting. Even better, he'd have a wife bring the coffee up to him after he had started work. Maybe even his own wife. He tried to imagine what such a wife would look like. There were so many pretty women to choose from, but Daisy kept flicking up on his mental screen, standing there next to his easel, a steaming cup of coffee in her hand. Better yet, on a tray with two steaming cups of coffee and a plate of cookies! No point in skimping on a daydream. He glanced out at Daisy sitting at her desk in the briefing room. She was scratching an itch on her head with the lead point of a pencil. Hmm. He'd have to give this more thought.

Lurch appeared in his doorway. "Hope I'm not interrupting a good daydream, boss."

"Far from it, Lurch. You find anything at the library on either of our suspects?"

"Not much. But I talked to Vera Freedy about her history of the county. There used to be a Beeker ranch out next to the river south of Famine. Adam Beeker was the owner. He died about eighty years ago. The ranch was one of the largest in Idaho. The Beekers ran thousands of cattle on it, but a corporation back in New York owns the ranch now. It mostly grows trees."

"I didn't expect you to read a whole book on it, Lurch."

"I didn't. I talked to Vera about it, and she told me about the Beekers. She said she had a whole chapter about the ranch."

"Interesting. I may head out to the ranch tomorrow. You want to go?"

"Naw, there might be shooting."

"I hope so."

"That all for me, boss?"

"No. See what you can turn up on the corporation that owns the ranch and ask Vera if she knows of any place on the ranch Beeker and Dance might hide out."

"Stupid of me to ask." Lurch headed back to his corner.

Tully grabbed a phone book, thumbed through it, found the number he wanted and dialed.

A gruff voice answered. "Yeah?"

"Batim, it's Bo Tully." Batim Scragg was one of the deadliest human beings in all of Idaho, possibly on the planet.

"Whatcha want, Bo?"

"You know what I want, Batim."

"I ain't takin' him back. Besides, that pretty girl you got livin' with you loves him, and he loves her. He don't try to bite her or anything. What happened, Bo, he started chompin' my chickens. Got a dozen of them running around with bare hind ends sticking out. Ever time I see Clarence he's got a mouthful of feathers."

Tully groaned. "Listen, Batim, all you need to do is build a hen house and a chicken-wire pen, and Clarence couldn't get near them."

"Wouldn't work, Bo. These are free-range chickens, and I ain't penning them up to keep them safe from your little dog."

Tully leaned back in his chair and rolled his eyes. "I'll tell you what, Batim, I'll be over in Famine tomorrow, and we'll discuss it then."

"Don't bring Clarence!"

"Why I called in the first place, I'm looking for a couple of men I think may be hanging out over around Famine."

"Wouldn't be them bank robbers, would it?"

"Yes, it would. Suspected bank robbers. We don't have any proof they're the ones robbed the bank and shot a young fellow up on Chimney Rock Mountain, but they're all I've got right now."

"I heard about it on the radio."

"Well, my suspects vanished. I figure they might have holed up somewhere over around Famine and maybe stayed there while they were setting up the robbery, if they set up the robbery. If we can find such a place, we may be able to get some leads on them."

Batim said, "Durned if I don't miss crime, Bo. I just got too old for it."

Tully laughed. "Yeah, I'm getting too old for it myself, Batim."

"So what else you want, Bo?"

"You know anybody in the area around Famine with the names of either Dance or Beeker?

The old man was quiet for a moment. Tully hoped he was turning the names over in his mind. Then Batim said, "There's a big old brick mansion out on the river. Nobody lives in it anymore. Years ago a fire pretty much gutted it. It's huge, three or more stories high, all red brick. Must have five big chimneys on it. Folks still call the area the Beeker Ranch. Use to be said a cowboy could ride in a straight line for a week and never be off the ranch. An old couple, Alma and Harold, live in an old double-wide mobile home near the burnt-out mansion. I guess their job is to look after what's left of it, or maybe because they don't have anywhere else to live. I think Alma is somehow related to the Beeker what started the ranch. I'm pretty sure her last name used to be Beeker. Both Alma and Harold are crazy as bedbugs, but nice enough. Most crazy folks I know are nice. Maybe that's what makes them crazy, they can't find any of their own kind."

Tully smiled. "Maybe you should go into psychiatry, Batim."

"Maybe. But I got a policy never to go into anything I can't spell. Anyway, your pal Dave Perkins, the fake Indian, was out there hunting pheasants or something last fall and asked Alma if she could give him a drink of water. She said maybe he'd prefer a nice glass of lemonade. Dave said sure and sat down on a chopping block out in the yard, and pretty soon Alma comes out with a glass of green lemonade. Dave takes a big swig and thanks her. Then he asks, 'How'd you get your lemonade that nice green color?' She said, 'Oh, I just dump in some of Harold's aftershave. Makes it pretty and tastes fine too, don't it?'"

Tully laughed. "Good thing Dave survived? I may need to use him tomorrow."

Batim cackled. "Yeah, Dave says it's the best lemonade he ever drunk!"

Tully thanked Batim for the information and said he might stop by and see him tomorrow.

"That be fine, Bo. Just don't bring Clarence. If you need a little back up on your hunt for the criminals, I'm pretty handy with a gun."

"I know you are, Batim. If it starts to look like a tough situation, I'll give you a call. I plan on using Dave for any tough situations, though. And I may bring along an FBI agent."

"An FBI agent! I hate the FBI!"

"This one's a pretty woman."

"They got pretty women FBI agents?"

"Yes, they do. I may stop by and show her to you."

"I'd be mighty pleased if you do. Nothing I like better than pretty women. Just don't bring Clarence."

Chapter 11

Tully stopped at Angie's hotel at eight the next morning. Clarence was on the front seat beside him, a seat belt looped around his middle. Angie was watching for Bo out the front window of the hotel. She came out, opened the car door and started to get in.

"Clarence! What are you doing here?"

The little dog wagged his tail.

Tully said, "I'm returning him to his rightful owner."

"Oh, that's too bad, Bo." She scratched Clarence behind the ears and started fumbling around for her seat belt. The dog wagged his tail. He must like women, Tully thought.

"You should keep him, Bo. Give you some company in that empty, old house of yours."

"I can provide all the company I need in my empty, old house. You want him, Angie?"

"Really, Bo. You'd give him to me? What about his rightful owner?"

Tully laughed. "His rightful owner will probably just shoot him, if Clarence keeps chomping his chickens."

"Maybe I will take him home with me," Angie said. "I could use a little company at my own empty house."

Tully drove over to his father's mansion on a hill overlooking the town of Blight. Pap Tully had been one of the most corrupt sheriffs in Blight County's long history of corrupt sheriffs, most of them Tullys. Bo was the exception to the family tradition of corruption, causing his father to regard him as dimwitted and something of a disgrace.

"I hope you don't mind, Angie, I'm asking my father to go along with us. He can be a considerable help, if a dangerous situation develops."

"Mind?" she said. "Bo, I love Pap!"

"I thought you might. He affects most women that way. I think women must have a weakness for vile old men."

"How about vile young men?"

"Not so much."

Reaching the end of the long driveway that led up the mountain to Pap's house, Tully honked the horn. A few seconds later Pap emerged from the front door carrying a pump shotgun in one hand and a lever-action rifle in the other. His beautiful housekeeper, Deedee, came out on the porch and waved to them. Tully gave her a smile, and Deedee smiled even broader and waved back. Pap opened the hatch door of the Explorer and stowed the guns in the cargo area, then walked around and climbed into the back seat.

"I was looking forward to sitting with Angie," he said, "but I see you got an extra passenger."

Clarence turned and growled at him.

"Miserable little mutt," Pap said. "What you gonna to do with him, Bo?"

"I'm returning him to his rightful owner, Batim Scragg."

"Serves both of them right," Pap muttered. He fussed with his seat belt and then threw it aside. Tully had been watching him in the rearview mirror.

"Put it on!" he ordered.

The old man finally got the buckle to snap shut. "The worst invention humans ever come up with," he growled. "Just another modern contrivance to pester us with."

Tully shook his head. "I don't know why it is that old people can't figure out how to fasten their seat belts." He turned around in the driveway and headed back down the hill. "I see you brought one of your pump shotguns. How come not an automatic?"

"Because when you might be shootin' at humans, the pump gives you a bit longer to think. You reckon we might actually catch up to those bank robbers over in Famine, Bo?"

"I doubt it, Pap. I suspect they're long gone. But we might find some evidence and maybe get a lead on where we can track them down, provided we can find the cabin they were staying in. An old couple is still living on a portion of what used to be the Beeker Ranch. They've got a double-wide mobile home next to the remains of the old mansion. Batim told me the woman's name used to be Beeker or maybe still is. That's the name of one of our suspects."

Pap said, "I know that ranch, Bo. So you figure maybe the suspects holed up there for a while? Maybe they're still there. Good thing I brought the pump.

No need killing anybody who don't need killing. You know something, Bo, that ranch ain't nothing like what it was when I was a kid. It was thousands and thousands of acres of grazing land and timber. As I recollect, the owner and his wife was murdered in the mansion. Your great-grandfather Tully was the sheriff back then, and he hung a couple of the fellas who might have been the murderers. It was the sensible thing to do in those days, just in case the fellers you caught was the ones what done it. I hear the mansion's been haunted ever since."

"Haunted!" Angie said. "You don't believe in ghosts do you, Pap?"

"I try not to, Angie, but I like to cover my bases. I wouldn't even think about spending a night in the mansion, that being my first base."

Tully laughed. "Too bad, Pap. I brought along a blanket for you, just in case we do decide to spend the night in there."

Pap chuckled. "If you spend the night there, you can find me at Dave's place in Famine the next morning."

"Surely you're not going to let me and Angie spend the night there alone. It would be indecent. You know how people talk. You would ruin the Tully name."

"The Tully name's been ruined for a hundred years," Pap said. "And you ain't done nothin' to improve it."

Pap dug out the makings of one of his hand-rolled cigarettes. "Speaking of improving the Tully name, Angie, I once was awarded a medal for bravery by the governor. How about that for improving the Tully name? I ever show you my medal?"

"Yes, you did, Pap, and it's beautiful!"

Tully glared up into the rearview mirror at Pap working on his cigarette fixings. "You touch that thing off, Pap, and Angie and I are going to open our windows and freeze you to death."

"Oh, all right!" He wadded up the hand-rolled and stuffed it in an ash tray. "I hate it when a son of mine turns into a little old lady."

Angie said, "Is it true that visiting Famine is like going back in time a hundred years?"

Tully and Pap burst out laughing. "More like two hundred," Tully said.

"Well, I think it will be a treat."

"If you're mighty low on treats," Pap said.

Tully added, "Blight City is an exotic metropolis compared with Famine. It's better now that I've put about half the population in prison. Some Faminites think that was the good half though."

Angie said, "I would never base my judgment on anything I hear from you two."

Pap snorted. "Don't put me in the same class with Bo, Angie. I can't stand the way he distorts and exaggerates."

Tully said, "Only because you prefer your own distortions and exaggerations. It does occur to me, Angie, that you and Dave Perkins hit it off a while back when you were up here helping me solve the huckleberry murders."

"*Helping*?" she said. "Well, I have to admit that Dave was like a breath of fresh air compared with you two. He was charming and intelligent and attentive."

"Attentive," Tully said. "I've been working on that one."

"Me too," Pap said. "But I gotta warn you, Angie, you might think Dave Perkins ain't nothin' more than an amiable nut, but he's about as deadly a critter as you're likely to run into around these parts."

"I've had some experience with him in that regard," she said.

"That's right, Angie!" said Pap. "I forgot! You seen him shoot, in the dark of night on a raft. His target tried to pick me off, but killing that sniper had no more effect on Dave than slapping a mosquito. If I had to guess, I'd say he'd done that sort of thing a few times before. He's kind of secretive about his past, don't you think, Bo?"

"Yeah, and I try not to press him on it."

Angie suddenly became serious. "You know something, Bo, that was my impression, too. I guess I expected Dave to be more disturbed or something, after killing that man."

Tully nodded. "Me too. Dave is a pretty easy-going fellow, but I make an effort not to rile him. If you want to date him, Angie, far be it from me to discourage you, just because he's a murderous maniac."

Angie sat in silence, a thoughtful expression on her face.

Tully smiled.

An hour later they approached the little town of Famine. Tully slowed and turned off on the road leading into Batim Scragg's ranch. Batim was standing on the back porch. As he walked over to the car, Angie rolled down her window. "Hi, Mr. Scragg . . ." In that instant Clarence wiggled loose from his seat belt and leaped out the window, landing in the arms of Batim Scragg and licking his grizzled face. The startled old man reached up and began scratching the back of the little dog's neck. "I thought I told you not to bring Clarence, Bo."

Tully held up his arms in a gesture of helplessness. "I didn't intend to, Batim. I was just taking him along for the ride. Shove him back through the window, and we'll take him with us."

Clarence licked Batim's cheek again. The old man continued scratching the back of Clarence's neck. "To tell you the truth, Bo, I'm actually glad to see the little fellow. I got a pen only halfway done for the chickens, but you can let him stay."

"I didn't mean to foist him off on you, Batim. Just stuff him back in here."

"No! It's all right, Bo. He's stayin' here."

"Well, okay, if you insist."

Back on the highway, Pap said, "You oughta be ashamed of yourself, Bo, pullin' a trick like that on a senile old man."

"Senile! No way Batim Scragg is senile. You'd have to be senile to think he's senile. He just knows a fine dog when he sees one."

Angie smiled. "I suspected something when Clarence started wagging his tail the moment we turned in the driveway. I'm not sure if that's an evil streak you have, Bo, or something else."

Tully glanced at her. "I prefer to think of it as evil."

"You would," she said.

As they entered the little town of Famine, Tully acted as tour guide, pointing out the three bars, the gas station, the grocery store, the post office and, finally, Famine's claim to fame, Dave's House of Fry. "People come from all over the world to eat here," he told Angie as they turned into the parking lot, past the sign that said, "World's Biggest and Best Chicken-Fried Steak," and a bit farther on, "World's Smallest Indian Reservation."

"I hope you haven't eaten breakfast yet, Angie, because I have a real treat for you."

Pap laughed. "Don't let him fool you. Dave never charges us for breakfast or anything else. That's one reason Bo likes the place so much."

Tully said, "Dave only pretends to be an Indian, but he's actually the best tracker I've ever come across."

"Yep," Pap said. "Tracking is practically a lost art these days. To find someone as good as Dave is pretty amazing."

Angie said, "You forget, I've seen him in action. You know, it might not be a bad idea to take Dave along when we go looking for the bad guys."

Pap laughed. "Bo's way ahead of you on that one, Angie."

"Hey," Tully said. "I can handle the bad guys without Dave."

As usual, the Famine breakfast crowd had packed the restaurant, and the roar of voices was deafening. A cloud of cigarette, cigar, and pipe smoke wafted among the tables. Suddenly a waitress appeared out of the smoke, a cigarette dangling from her lips.

"Tiffany!" Tully exclaimed

"Bo! I ain't seen you here in a coon's age. Booth or table? I'll clear out some of our locals for you."

"Oh, better not do that, Tiff. I need all the votes I can get."

"Hey, Sheriff!" a man in a booth called out. "We was just finishin' up. You can have this one."

"Why thanks, pardner. Don't mean to rush you." Tully shook the man's hand, gave his wife a hug, and patted the two kids on the head.

"See that?" Pap whispered to Angie. "Them kids ain't even old enough to vote yet."

"I took note of that," Angie whispered back. "He may be the best politician I've ever seen."

Holding a dishpan up to the table with her knee, Tiffany swept the dirty plates off the table in two swipes of her dishrag, made two more swipes, and the table was clean. Pap and Tully scooted into one side of the booth and Angie into the other.

Angie said, "Bo, I noticed you suddenly changed into the folk vernacular when you spoke to that man."

"I did?" he said. "What's a vernacular?"

Angie laughed. "I've heard you do it before, whenever you pretended to be one of the guys." She spoke in a deep voice, imitating Tully. "S'cuse me, pawdner, while Ah stomp this cow manure offen maw boots, and Ah'll set a spell with you."

Tully looked around to make sure they weren't being overheard. "You better shut up, Angie. You could cost me the next election right here."

She laughed. "Did I do him about right, Pap?"

The old man was almost doubled over with laughter. "You nailed him, Angie."

Tiffany reappeared with three large menus which she flopped onto the table. "Coffee all 'round?"

"You bet," Tully said.

"'You bet!'" Angie squealed after the waitress left. "Bo, you're killing me!"

"I'm about to. Now shut up about my vernacular. Here comes Tiff."

The waitress clunked three large cups on the table and filled them with coffee. Then she fished into her apron pocket and brought out a handful of cream containers and dumped them on the table. She stared at Angie, who was trying to wipe away the tears running down her face. "Anything wrong?"

Tully said, "It's just that we're expecting a death in the near future."

"Sorry to hear it," Tiffany said. "You want to order now?"

All three took The World's Biggest and Best Chicken-Fried Steak.

Dave Perkins strolled over. His long gray hair, braided into a thick coil, ran down his back halfway to his belt. Although there was plenty of room in the booth, he slid his hip tightly up against Angie's. She didn't move away, Tully noticed.

Dave said, "I'd have come over sooner if I'd noticed Angie was here. I thought it was just you two galoots."

"I guess you don't need an introduction," Tully said.

"Nope," Dave said. "We don't."

Tully said, "Usually I have better sense than to expose a beautiful woman to you, Dave, but Angie is here because we're on serious business."

"Yeah, and I know what it is. You're after your murderer and some bank robbers."

Tully told Dave about the Beeker woman at the mobile home and the Beeker Ranch.

"Interesting," Dave said. "I've met the Beeker woman. Could be a connection. Not much to go on though."

Their food arrived. Angie expressed her amazement at the size of the chicken-fried steaks.

"Try the hash browns," Dave said. "They're also the best in the world."

She tried a forkful. "Oh yum! They are so good, Dave!"

"They're not quite there yet. I'm tinkering with the celery and onions and a couple of different spices."

Tully had to admit the hash browns were also the best in the world. He sometimes drove all the way to Famine for the hash browns alone.

"So how come you know why we're here?" Pap said.

"Bo's friend stopped by and said he was checking out some leads for the sheriff."

"Friend?" Tully said. "What friend is that?"

"I forget the name, but he's built like a splitting maul . . ."

"Gridley Shanks!" Tully and Angie said in unison.

Dave looked from one to the other. "Well, is he friend or not, Bo? He knew Angie and that she was with the FBI and said both of you would be showing up soon."

"You tell him anything, Dave?" Angie asked.

"No. Didn't know anything to tell him. I try not to get involved with the locals any more than to take their money. He asked if I minded his talking to some of the regulars, and I said no, go ahead. He seemed to get an earful from them. Of course they talk just to talk, whether they know anything or not."

"You have any idea what he asked them?"

"No." Dave turned and looked around the dining room. Then he yelled, "Harry, come over to our table for a second, will you?"

A skinny white-haired man in overalls reluctantly put down his knife and fork and walked over. Dave, introduced him to the others. Angie reached around Dave and shook his hand.

"The FBI!" shouted Harry.

Tully said, "Shhh. She's working undercover. We don't want everyone to know the FBI is in town. There would be an instant mass exodus."

"Ma'am, excuse me if I'm kind of nervous," Harry said. "You're the first FBI agent I ever touched. I didn't even realize they made pretty ones."

"Why, thank you, Harry. I wish I ran into more gentlemen like you. But what we need to know is if there are any Beekers living around here."

Harry thought for a moment. "None to speak of. Beekers used to be thick as fleas around here, but they all moved away or died off. There is one of the Beeker girls left. She ain't a girl anymore, come to think of it. She must be eighty or ninety by now. Her and her husband live on a portion of the old Beeker Ranch. Don't see much of them. Pretty much keep to themselves. Odd you should be curious about the Beekers. A fella come by last night asking about them."

"You tell him anything?"

"Just what I told you."

"Well, thanks, Harry," Angie said. "We'd better be getting out to the Beeker Ranch while there's a Beeker left."

"If there still is one," Tully muttered.

Dave told Harry his chicken-fried steak was on the house.

"Why, thank you, Dave. You never done that before."

"Won't do it again, Harry."

Pap picked up the coffee thermos and refilled all their cups.

"So what's the plan now?" Dave asked.

"I've got a really bad feeling about our Gridley Shanks," Tully said.

"You think he's connected to the murder and robbery?" Pap asked.

Tully shoved his half-eaten steak away. "He seems connected to every part of it. I brought all of this up to him, and he said it was a convergence of incidentals, meaning every time I picked up a new fact, it coincidentally pointed at him. In addition to the convergence of incidentals, I think he's the mastermind behind both the robbery and the murder. I wouldn't even rule him out as the shooter. It all goes back to a partial fingerprint on a strip of flagging tape."

"Oh, no!" Angie gasped. "You can't mean it, Bo! You can't mean Grid was responsible for both the robbery and the murder."

"I hate it as much as you do, Angie. I thought I had him cold once, but I had leaped to a conclusion that was totally wrong. Dave, get yourself armed and come with us. This seems to be turning into a very dangerous situation."

"Am I still deputized, Bo?"

"No, but if you shoot anybody, I'll fix it up later."

"The Blight way!" Angie said. "I really hate overhearing these things."

Chapter 12

Dave slipped a rifle into the cargo area of the Explorer and got into the back seat with Pap. Angie sat up front with Tully. Pap said, "I'll tell you something about Famine I bet you don't know, Bo."

"Okay," Tully said, "even though I can't think of anything about Famine I want to know. Go ahead, Pap."

"You'll want to know this," Pap said. "Back when your great-grandfather Tully was sheriff of Blight County, Famine was called Beeker. I'd forgotten it myself, until that fella started talking about the place being overrun with Beekers. That's because the ranch was so big, hundreds of thousands of acres, it had its own town. Even had a hotel. Most of the hands lived in town, some with their own houses, some at the hotel. On the hill back of town is the old cemetery. You go up there, you'll find all kinds old grave markers that belong to Beekers and other ranch hands that got themselves killed on the ranch or in gunfights in town or just got too old. Famine was a right interesting place in those days. I hate that I missed it."

Tully glanced at him in the rearview mirror. "How come they changed the name from Beeker to Famine?"

"Gold. They had a gold rush. Folks rushed into town by the hundreds. Some of them even found gold and went away rich. After the rush came a famine. So that's what they called the town. Beeker still controlled everything."

Tully said, "I've always wanted a nice little gold mine. Nothing lavish, you understand. Just a modest little operation I could run by myself. The kind where you sort of pick up nuggets off the ground."

Pap said, "I had a gold mine once, me and Pinto Jack did. One time a bear . . ." Pap's head fell over on Dave's shoulder and he began to snore.

Dave said, "He always falls asleep when he gets to the part about the bear. One of these days I might actually find out where that mine was or at least what the bear did."

Tully said, "Yeah, I'd be happy finding out just what happened with the bear."

A short way out of town they ran into the intersection of the River Road between Blight and Famine. It looked so rough he couldn't imagine why anyone would use it, except to avoid the law. The road from Famine to the Beeker Ranch wasn't much better. It had almost petered out entirely when they turned in next to the mansion. The burnt-out structure gaped ominously over the river. Tully turned the Explorer around and parked next to an old double-wide mobile home set off to one side of the mansion. A wobbly line of wooden utility poles led down the road to one side of the double-wide. Even though it was still daylight, a light shone inside the front window of the home. They could hear a radio pounding out country with several singers wailing over the top of the guitars. Tully got out and knocked on the door. No answer. He looked around, thinking maybe the couple was working outside, but he could see no one. A fairly new pickup truck was parked nearby. He knocked again. Still no response. He tugged on his mustache, contemplating what to do next. His hand slipped beneath his vest and released the strap on the Colt Commander. He looked back at the car. His passengers stared at him in grim silence. He tried the door knob. It turned loosely, but then he noticed the door latch was missing. He pulled open the door. A white-haired woman wearing a pink nightgown lay on the floor, a bunny-rabbit slipper on one foot, its mate next to her. An elderly man lay in the middle of the floor. He wore only a pair of white long underwear. Both the man and the woman had been shot several times. A bungee cord dangled from the door, apparently the means by which the couple held the door shut. Tully stepped around a puddle of blood and crossed the room. He squatted down and felt the man's neck for a pulse but, as expected, found none. There was no point in checking the woman. After shutting off the light he hooked the bungee cord to a hook screwed into the wall, went outside and let the door close.

He took out his phone and called Daisy. "Hi, sweetheart."

She sighed into the phone. "You never call me that unless the news is bad."

"I'm afraid it is. There's a double-wide mobile home parked out here near a burnt-out mansion on the old Beeker place. Inside the double-wide are the bodies of an elderly man and woman. Both shot several times. I cannot for the life of me think of any reason someone would kill them. They appear perfectly harmless, no weapons in sight or anything like that. They seem to have been needlessly murdered in cold blood. So I need Susan and her M.E. people out here pronto."

"Right, boss, I'll get them on their way. Will you be there to meet them?"

"Yes, I think so. Tell them to inquire at the gas station in Famine, and the lady there will point them to the road that leads to the Beeker place. Now get me Lurch."

Lurch said, "You've got me, boss. I already picked up."

"Good. I'm going to need you out here with your CSI kit as soon as you can make it. First, did you get hold of the lady who wrote a whole chapter on the Beeker Ranch in her Blight County history."

"Yeah, Vera Freedy."

"Any chance you could bring her?"

"She's pretty frail-looking, but my feeling is she would be hot to trot if she had a chance to get in on a murder investigation."

"Good. Get hold of her as quick as you can, and haul her out here. I have some important questions for her. If you hurry, you can ride out with Susan and her people."

"Great, boss. Just so I don't have to ride back with them. On the other hand, I think I'll bring my own Explorer."

"Suit yourself. Tell Pugh and Thorpe I need them out here, too. Everybody come armed to the teeth, vests, everything. Daisy, you still there?"

"Still here, boss."

"Anything going on?"

"Same ole, same ole."

"That bad, huh. Well, I'll probably be out here another day or two. So you're in charge."

"Good. I'll shake up the troops while you're gone. Be careful out there, boss."

"I'm always careful, sweetheart." He beeped off.

When he got back in the Explorer, Dave said, "You look pretty serious, Bo. I take it the occupants of the double-wide weren't too helpful."

"Afraid not. Both of them shot dead. An old couple. Totally senseless murders. No way they could have threatened anybody."

Dave scratched his chin. "Maybe they just posed a possible threat."

Angie said, "They could have known something the killer didn't want known. Could you tell how long they've been dead?"

"No, but I've got the M.E. on her way."

Pap suddenly jerked upright. "I just remembered something about the mansion. "I was out here when I was about twenty. My friend Richy Walker and me was canoeing the river down from where his folks farmed, about ten miles up from a foot bridge that crossed the river near here. I figured it would take us three or four hours to get down to the highway bridge."

Dave said, "You can't cover that distance in three or four hours in a canoe."

"Now you tell me, Dave. That's what we discovered the hard way. It got dark before we were halfway here. And creepy, too, with patches of fog hanging low over the water. Most of the way the river was bordered by old forests on both sides, mostly giant cottonwoods. We was both exhausted, but no way was we going to pull over to the bank and spend the night. The footbridge is upriver about a quarter mile from here, and we almost got out there to walk the rest of the way. Then we came to this clearing, and that's when we saw the mansion. It just rose up out of the darkness with all those big gaping windows busted out, and weeds and vines growing up around it. Even in the dark you could tell the inside of it had burnt out and that it was haunted. If ever there was a place for ghosts to hang out, this was it. The one thing now stands out in my mind, there was wide concrete steps going down into the river. It was like at one time somebody went swimming there and needed special access to the water. We stopped next to the steps. That's when the sound of someone playing a piano came drifting out from inside the mansion. I tell you, I stood that canoe up on its rear end for the next mile down river. Richy was flailing away with his paddle, too, but I had him too high up to reach the water. Finally, we got too exhausted even to hold a paddle. I don't know about Richy, but I couldn't get my hair to lay down for a week."

Angie said, "I'm sure there's a rational explanation to the piano music you heard drifting down from the burnt-out shell of a building."

"There is," Tully said. "A ghost was in there playing a ghost piano."

Angie sighed. "Strange, I didn't think of that."

Dave said, "If the mansion was already gutted out when you were twenty, I'm surprised it's still standing. You'd think one of the owners would have called in a crane or at least a big dozer to knock it down."

"Maybe they did," Tully said. "And the dozer driver heard piano music coming from inside. How much speed can you get out of a dozer anyway, Dave?"

"Not nearly enough to suit me, if I heard a ghost playing a ghost piano in there."

Pap said, "I remember something my daddy once told about the Beeker Ranch. He was sheriff then and knew Beeker. He was driving out to see the old man about something, mostly just to check on him, I think, because Beeker had started to lose touch with reality. As he was leaving the ranch, Pappy noticed a huge field littered with hay bales. He said there must have been thousands of bales out there, stretching away as far as he could see. Rising up over the Hoodoo Mountains was a huge black storm cloud, and he realized all those bales was about to be ruined by rain. It was late in the evening on a Saturday, so Pappy rushed into town and over to the bingo parlor, because he knew most of the people in Famine would be in there playing bingo. He ran inside, stepped on a chair and up onto a table and shouted, 'A big rainstorm is coming and Beeker has thousands of hay bales out in the open!'"

Tully imagined all the people in the bingo parlor rushing in long streams of trucks, pickups, trailers, wagons, and even cars, anything that might carry a few bales to somehow save the hay. "So what happened?"

"The folks just laughed and went on with their bingo game."

"Good heavens!" Angie said. "Was all the hay ruined?"

Pap paused, as though recollecting the details of the event. "The hay got rained on all right, but just enough to ferment it."

Tully raised a hand. "Stop!"

Pap went on. "But all the cows in Blight Country ate it anyway. Their milk turned out to be about twenty proof, and the school kids thought it was the best milk they ever drunk."

His audience groaned.

Pap said, "My daddy wouldn't lie about a thing like that."

Tully laughed. "So he wasn't anything like you. I think I have an explanation for the piano music though. It was probably coming from a radio in what we used to call a trailer house, parked about where the big double-wide is."

Dave said, "I prefer to think it was ghosts."

"Me too," Angie said.

Pap stretched and yawned. "So what we gonna do now, Bo? Sit here all night thinking up stories?"

Tully stroked his mustache. "I don't really know. This is a crime scene, and we're not leaving here until it's secure. I've got Susan and the Unit on their way out. Maybe they can come up with something to explain why anyone would kill an old couple. I myself don't have a clue. Anybody here have an idea?" He looked around. "Just what I thought. Zip. I don't know why I drag you all along."

Pap said, "Maybe just to torment us."

"No, there was another reason. Ah, yes, you mentioned there was a footbridge crossing the river a ways from here. How far do you think it was, Pap?"

Pap scratched his jaw. "Been a long time, Bo. Let me think. I'd guess it wasn't more than half a mile upstream."

"While we're waiting for Susan, I think I'll check it out. It might have washed out years ago."

Dave said, "I could use a little exercise myself. I'll go with you, Bo."

They walked into the woods behind the double-wide, mostly second-growth fir and pine and a few tamaracks, fairly scraggly as woods go. They walked down toward the river in search of a trail but found none.

Dave said, "You'd think if there was a bridge across the river, there would at least be a trail leading to it from the mansion."

"Yeah," Tully said. "I doubt the bridge has been used in fifty years. It probably washed out long ago."

Dave pointed to a mountain rising up steeply from the river's edge on the far side. "What I can't understand is why anyone would want to cross the river in the first place. The mountains goes practically straight up on the other side."

They came to a small clearing and suddenly there was the bridge, arcing up over the river."

"Wow," Tully said. "That's a pretty fancy bridge to be tucked away back here in the woods, with no obvious use."

Dave pointed across the river. "There's a trail going up the mountain but it would be a pretty steep climb."

Tully stepped up on the end of the bridge. "Yeah, I can see half a dozen switchbacks from here. Somebody put in a lot of effort, building that trail. The bridge still looks fairly sturdy, Dave. Why don't you walk across and see if you notice anything?"

"Your idea, Bo."

"You remember what Pap said about Famine having a gold rush years ago?"

"Yeah but I'm still not walking across the bridge, Bo."

"Might be a nice little gold mine up on the mountain someplace."

"You go take a look. If you find a nice little gold mine, we'll split it fifty-fifty."

Tully laughed. "Not a chance." He worked his way gingerly across the bridge, which creaked and groaned a little more than he liked. The switchbacks made the climb up the mountain a good deal easier. He was about to turn back when he came to the mine entrance. He had to squat down to peer into it. The tunnel went back into the mountain a dozen yards, stopping at what appeared to be a cave in. Water was leaking down near the entrance. He straightened up and look around. A small log shelter squatted off to one side. Whoever started the mine must have thought it worth the effort to build something to stay in. He walked over and peered inside. There were signs someone had spent some time in it recently, an empty lunch sack and a potato-chip bag. He turned around and made his way back down the trail and across the bridge.

Dave asked, "Find anything, Bo?"

"Naw. A trail leading nowhere."

"I bet. Just remember, we split fifty-fifty if you hit the mother lode."

"You'll be the first person I call, Dave. Maybe that mine was the reason the old couple was killed. It did look as if somebody had been fooling around in there. A really stupid person because it looked as if the ceiling could collapse at any moment. So, Dave, how come you knew about the mine?"

"I came across it five years ago, when I was back here on furlough. The cave-in kind of discouraged me from exploring very far in. But somebody had to have a reason for digging it in the first place."

Tully checked his watch. "Susan should be at the mansion pretty soon. We had better get back."

Chapter 13

After exploring the woods for an hour, they got back to the mansion just as the medical examiner's two vans were pulling in.

Susan rolled down a window and smiled. "You look rode hard and put away wet, Bo."

"Good. That must mean I'm still alive, which is more than I can say for the old couple in the double-wide over there."

"Murdered, I take it."

"Yeah, multiple gunshot wounds, no weapon in sight. Senseless. It will be a great help if you can determine when they were killed."

Susan climbed out of the van and stretched. "I'll get right to it, Bo."

"Good." He walked back to the sheriff's department Explorer parked behind the M.E.'s van.

Brian Pugh got out of the passenger side. "So we have a double murder, boss."

"Yeah, an old couple. I can't think of any reason to rob them. Their total wealth probably didn't amount to more than their last Social Security checks."

Ernie Thorpe got out of the rear seat.

"You fellas bring rifles?" Tully asked.

Ernie said, "Armed to the teeth, boss."

Pugh shook his head. "These days a Social Security check is more than enough to get a person murdered."

"Yeah, I guess you're right about that," Tully said. "But I don't think they were killed for their money."

"What then?"

"Probably to shut them up. About what I have no idea."

Lurch got out of the second Explorer, walked around and opened the rear passenger door. A gray-haired lady stepped out and walked stiffly over to Tully. Lurch introduced her. "Boss, this is Vera Freedy. She's the one who wrote the chapter about the Beeker Ranch. Miss Freedy, this is . . ."

"Oh, Byron, I know who Sheriff Bo Tully is. Everybody in Blight County knows Sheriff Tully."

Tully shook the lady's hand. "Miss Freedy, please accept my apology for Lurch, uh, Byron, dragging you all the way out to a murder scene."

"Sheriff, it wasn't Byron's fault at all. I insisted on coming when he told me it involved the old Beeker Ranch. I'm something of a local historian, and I couldn't resist a chance to visit the place even if it involved the murders of its caretakers."

"Vera, maybe you can shed some light on our situation here. Before our robbery suspects became robbery suspects, they indicated they had found a place to stay over by Famine. One of them was named Horace Beeker, so that led us to the old Beeker Ranch, which as you can see is now used to grow trees rather than cattle. Lurch, uh, I mean Byron . . ."

"'Lurch' is fine with me, Sheriff. I like it better than Byron."

"Good. Anyway, Lurch told me you had recently written about the Beeker Ranch, and I thought maybe, if you can remember, there might have been some mention of cabins or some other place where the ranch hands stayed."

"I'm sorry, Sheriff, but there was no mention of such a place. All the hands lived in the little town of Beeker, now called Famine. As you may know, the Beekers were not highly thought of by the local population, probably not unusual for rich landowners, particularly rich landowners who build empires the local population depends on."

"I suspected as much, Vera, but I was hoping you might have come across something while researching the Beekers."

"I did, actually, something that may be of help to you, Sheriff. Mr. Beeker was not totally bad to his employees and the townspeople. Every year he put on a huge picnic everyone was invited to, even all the forest service personnel in the region. The forest rangers contributed canned hams and all kinds of other food left over from feeding firefighters. Alcoholic beverages flowed freely, and half a dozen bands came out from Blight City to supply music. People danced and sang till the sun came up in the morning."

Tully said, "Sounds like a good time was had by all."

"Yes, I'm sure, but I think what may be of interest to you in your investigation, Sheriff, was where the picnic was held."

"Really? Where?"

"On Round Top Mountain."

"Round Top? I've heard of it. But why would it interest me?"

"It had a forest service lookout tower on it. I believe the tower is still there. The forest service has done away with most of the towers, but I'm writing a history of them. They're fascinating. Anyway, the Round Top tower still exists, or did last year when I was working on my book. It would be a great place for outlaws to hang out."

Tully stared at her in disbelief. He suddenly remembered something Ed Dance had said, only to be hushed up by Beeker. Dance had blurted out the only thing their cabin came with was a view. "You didn't happen to bring a map showing the road to Round Top, did you, Vera?"

"I'm afraid not, Bo. I imagine the road is long gone. I doubt you can even find any evidence of it."

Tully tugged on the droopy corner of his mustache. "Here's what I think, Vera. The men who killed the old couple in the double-wide over there did so because they didn't want us to find out about the tower on Round Top. Somehow the killers knew about the tower and are hiding out there, until they think they can slip away. Maybe the Beeker woman told Horace Beeker about it, and he killed her."

"But, Sheriff, if the road is gone, how are you going to find the way to the lookout? I know Round Top is on the highest range of the Hoodoo Mountains, but I don't have a clue how to get there."

Tully smiled. "Don't worry about that. I just happen to have the world's greatest tracker along. If our killers left any trail at all, he'll find it."

Chapter 14

Tully heard the tracker shout that he had found several sets of tire tracks. Dave strolled out of the woods. "The freshest one is the last to come out. One or more of our suspects may be long gone. I still haven't found any sign of a road. The tracks just wind in and out through the trees."

Tully walked over to Dave and looked at the tracks. "What do you make of them?"

Dave shook his head. "Not much. Looks to me as if the first vehicle had some vague idea about where it was going its first trip in. It wandered around quite a bit. Once it found the the right track, it made three trips in and two trips out. That would seem to mean some of the folks are still in there. What do you think, Bo?"

Tully studied the tracks. "It looks to me as if the people in the first vehicle tried to brush out the first part of their tracks with branches or something. Once the driver of the second vehicle found the tracks of the first one, he didn't bother hiding his own tracks. I figure the occupants of one of those vehicles shot the old couple to keep them from telling about the hideout. The old woman was a Beeker, if Batim Scragg is correct. So maybe she recognized Horace Beeker. That might be reason enough for either Beeker or Dance to kill her. The old man was just an eyewitness to her murder and had to be disposed of too."

Susan walked over from the double-wide "So far I've checked only one body. My best estimate is she was killed three days ago, maybe even a little earlier. It's been pretty cold in there, so I'm mostly guessing."

Tully said, "Two days or earlier fits my time frame. I think their killers may be where we can find them. If you can manage it Susan, you might want to stick around for awhile, save you from making a trip back here."

"You think there might be more bodies?"

"That's my intention."

"I assume you're talking about the monsters that killed the old couple."

"Yeah. According to the tracks, they're still in there, unless they rode out with the second vehicle."

Susan said, "I'll send the two bodies we have here back to Blight and follow you in the other van with a couple of assistants. Don't expect any backup from my guys in a firefight. Following you always turns out to be a big mistake."

Tully smiled. "Not always, you have to admit."

Susan smiled back. "I guess you're right about that, once or twice anyway."

The caravan of cars consisted of the two red sheriff department Explorers, followed by the M.E.'s van. Vera rode with Lurch and Angie in Tully's back seat, Dave alongside him in the front seat. Pap rode with Pugh and Ernie in the second vehicle. Dave pointed out the tracks to Tully as their vehicle bumped and slid among the trees. After half an hour the tracks veered sharply off toward the mountains. Soon they could see the Hoodoos rearing up in the morning sun, a blue background flickering through a line of yellow tamaracks. Dave pointed to a stream flowing out of a drainage in the mountains. "An old road winds up through there, but it doesn't look like anything we or anybody else could navigate. I doubt it goes to Round Top."

Tully drove through the shallow stream, the tires slipping on mossy rocks. "I see where our friends drove up the other bank there." The Explorer plowed up the bank and through a dense patch of brush.

Dave laughed. "Brush is always good for a car's finish. Gives it that natural look."

"Yeah," Tully said. "This Explorer's getting about as natural as it's possible to get." He glanced over his shoulder. Pugh's Explorer had tentatively dipped its front tires into the stream. Susan's van had stopped, apparently to survey the situation. Tully stopped to wait for them.

Dave opened his door. "I'll get out and look around a bit."

"Be my guest." Tully turned to the backseat. "How you doing back there, Vera?" She looked a bit frazzled.

"Bo, this is the most thrilling adventure I've ever had."

"I thought you'd prefer this to riding back to town in a medical examiner's van with two dead bodies."

Vera nodded. "This is wonderful, Bo. I haven't had this much excitement in years."

He watched out the back window as the other Explorer clawed its way up out of the creek. "I'm not sure what's in store for us up ahead. If there's any shooting, Vera, you hit the floor fast and stay there."

"Shooting! Oh, dear, I didn't think it could get any better than this! All my life, Bo, I've wanted to have an adventure, and now I'm having one."

Tully turned and smiled at her. "I'm pleased you're enjoying it."

Vera laughed. "Agent Phelps probably has adventures like this all the time."

Angie forced a smile. "Well, actually, Vera, only when I somehow find myself in the company of Sheriff Tully. He's a regular magnet for excitement."

Dave came walking out of the trees and climbed back into the Explorer. "You're not going to believe this, Bo, but I've found something that resembles a road. Has to be an old service road to the lookout. We've probably been driving along next to it for the last half hour."

"Must be. Apparently the folks whose tracks we've been following didn't know about it either. How do we get to it?"

Dave pointed. "Crank her hard to the right, Bo. It just up on the other side of that mound of rock and gravel."

The Explorer bumped and thumped and scraped over the mound, coming to rest in a facsimile of a road. It appeared as though a creek had used it as a bed for a number of years, scouring it down to great slabs of rock, but nevertheless offering better going than the forest had. Tully pulled ahead and waited for the other Explorer and the mortuary van to crash in behind them. He could see Susan in his rearview mirror shaking her head in exasperation.

Tully glanced over his shoulder. Angie was fast asleep. "You doing all right, Vera?"

She laughed. "Bo, this is the most fun I've had in years. I think we've landed on the road to the lookout. There is a little map in the book, and if I remember correctly the road should start winding up the mountain pretty soon."

"Great! Once we're on the mountain we should get hard rock under us, although the road already looks better."

Dave squinted ahead through the windshield. "We seem to have lost the tracks we were following, but we should pick them up before long, if we're on the right road."

The road was much smoother than the tracks among the trees had been. Shortly after the grade increased Tully could see where other vehicles had burst through the embankment to get to the road.

Dave said, "You notice there's a faint track going down the road, Bo?"

"No, I've been having too much fun wrestling the steering wheel."

Dave leaned far out his window. "As I suspected, one of the vehicles has gone out, using the road part way or at least until it disappears. So there should be only one vehicle left at the lookout."

Tully shook his head. "I have to admit again, Dave, you are absolutely amazing. I can hardly make out the road, let alone some faint track on it."

"That's because you're not a tracker, Bo." He turned toward the back seat. "I hope you don't mind shooting, Vera."

"You think there might be shooting, Dave? That would be wonderful! I'm almost eighty and never had a shooting."

Tully looked at Dave and smiled. Dave turned his attention back to Vera. "My point is, some of the shooting might be directed at us. So as soon as the first shot is fired, I want you to lie down on the floor and stay there until the shooting stops."

"That's what Sheriff Tully told me, too. Will I need a gun, Dave?"

"If you do, I'll toss you a pistol. Do you know how to click off the safety?"

"Honey, I've been around guns all my life. I've never actually shot anyone though, at least not on purpose." She laughed. "You'd make a wonderful comedian, Dave. I've never seen a funnier expression! No, I've never shot anyone, period."

Angie said, "I must have dozed off. What's all this talk about guns?"

The road suddenly took on a steeper incline, and they began to move up the mountain, sometimes climbing over piles of rock that had washed down from above. Occasionally Tully would attempt to drive around them, knocking other rocks off the road and into the canyon below.

Angie stretched so she could see down into the canyon. "Looks to me if we go over the edge, we'll be in good shape for the first three hundred feet or so, but then we'll touch down. After that it'll be much harder going."

Vera laughed. "You're just trying to worry Bo, isn't she, Dave?"

Tully said, "Worked on me, Angie."

Up ahead a stream of water poured off an overhanging cliff. The water thundered on the roof as they drove under it. Dave spun around in his seat. "What the . . .!"

Tully laughed. "Just washing off some of the mud we picked up driving through the woods."

"You might have to back up, and let me stand under it a while," Dave growled at him.

Vera burst into laughter. "I know what you mean, Dave!"

He turned and frowned at her. "Can't I get anything by you, Vera? You're suppose to be a proper, little old lady."

"I know, Dave, but mostly I'm just a little old lady. Just because I volunteer in a library, that doesn't mean I'm proper."

The higher they went on the mountain, the better the road became, but soon they were in snow, already several inches deep and still falling. Tully said, "This gets any deeper, Dave, we may have to chain up."

"You brought chains?"

"As sheriff of Blight County, I always carry chains, enough for all four wheels."

"There doesn't seem to be any place to turn around. So we can't go back. You think this Explorer can handle the snow?"

"With all four wheels chained up, it can climb trees, although I try to avoid that if I can."

Tully was beginning to see the curvature of the mountain's bald top. "I think we're going to make it, Dave." He stopped the Explorer. "Vera, there's a plastic crate in the cargo area with some bullet-proof vests in it. Dig out two of them and hand them up to Dave and me. Take the others for Lurch, yourself, and Angie. Fasten the Velcro strips so that you get it good and tight." Tully could tell he had just made Vera's day. In the rearview mirror he watched her put the vest on. It completely enveloped her. If she walked across a floor, her feet would barely stick out the bottom. He couldn't help but smile.

Vera looked at Angie. "Did I do it right?"

Angie smiled at her. "You did it perfect, Vera. Just remember what Bo said. At the first shot, you hit the floor, and stay there until I tell you it's okay to get up. Got it?"

"Got it, Angie."

Tully opened his door and got out. He could see the front end of the silver Land Rover poking out from the other side of the tower. The other Explorer growled up behind them and stopped. Tully waited for the M.E.'s van to arrive. He walked back and opened the hatch door to the cargo area and took out Dave's rifle and his own. Pap came up and claimed his. Angie was checking her automatic. She worked the slide to chamber a round.

Pap said, "The four of us going to walk up to the tower side by side like the shootout at the OK Corral?"

Tully said, "I don't think so. They could have heard us climbing the mountain for the last half hour. We have the road blocked, so there's no way they can get out. I suspect they'll be waiting for us. Angie, you and Pap take rifles and cover Dave and me as we move up toward the tower. That lookout cabin isn't going to give our friends up there much cover in a shootout, and I hope they know that. There's a walkway all around the cabin, and there are large windows on all four sides. In order to get a shot at Dave and me, they'll have to come out on the walkway. You know what to do if they come out armed. FBI, you'd better use Dave's rifle and let him use your automatic."

Angie handed the pistol to Dave and took his rifle.

"You know how to run one of these?" Dave asked Angie.

"Just point and shoot, right? It's been a while, but I can figure it out. Let's see, the bullet comes out the little round hole at the other end, right?"

Angie levered a shell into the chamber. She and Pap walked up to the front of the Explorer so they could brace their arms on the hood.

Walking cross the open area below the tower seemed to Tully like the longest walk he had ever taken in his life. The one good sign he noticed, no smoke came out of the cabin's chimney. Either the occupants were asleep or had somehow snuffed out the fire when they heard the little caravan coming up the mountain. They reached the tower stairs.

He glanced at Dave. "What do you think?"

"About what?"

"About climbing the stairs?"

Dave scratched his chin. "Well, Sheriff, now that I think about it, I'd like you to go first. I'll be right behind you, covering your butt."

"It's not my butt I'm worried about."

"What are you worried about? Usually, I'm not all that interested in your worries, but in this case, they might affect me."

"I'm worried about some ignoramus lunging out of the cabin and spraying these stairs with an automatic weapon."

Dave appeared to be turning this over in his mind. "In that case, maybe I should wait at the bottom of the tower."

Tully jerked his Colt Commander from his shoulder holster and started up the stairs, walking on the toes of his boots. He could hear Dave close behind, walking on the toes of his boots, even though the suspects could have heard them coming for the last hour. They reached the walkway with no threat from inside. Then Tully saw the cabin door had been kicked in, its glass broken, the wood frame splintered where the lock had been torn loose.

He stuck his boot out and shoved the door wide open. Snow had drifted in and left a streak of white across the floor. He stepped in quickly, pistol leveled, his finger on the trigger.

Horace Beeker and Ed Dance were seated on a cot, their heads leaning back against a window sill, their mouths gaping. Their upper halves were soaked with blood. Each had been shot multiple times. Beeker had a pistol clutched in his hand. Dance had one in his lap.

Tully straightened up. Dave walked up alongside him. "Well, I guess we didn't have to worry so much about these two."

Tully looked slowly around the cabin. "Well, no sign of the loot. I suspect that may have been the motive for killing our two friends here." Dave reached out with the automatic and used it to lift a jacket lying between Beeker and Dance. Another pistol was under the jacket. They had obviously been taken by surprise, eating a meager meal from a can of pork'n'beans they had been passing back and forth. Dirty spoons lay beside them.

"I'll probably never eat pork'n'beans again," Dave said.

"Me neither." Tully pointed at the pistols. "I suspect one of those was used to kill the old couple. What do you think, Dave?"

"You don't think the same guy did these two?"

"Could be, but I don't think so. Lurch should be able to tell us who shot whom, when we get the bullets from Susan. I suspect our dead friends here did the old couple, probably to keep us from knowing about the tower." He pointed to two rifles leaning against the wall. "If those are both seven millimeter, we may have the weapon that killed Vergil. Lurch should be able to figure out from the fingerprints which rifle belonged to Beeker and which to Dance, and then we'll know which one of them shot Vergil."

"You're pretty sure one of them did?"

"I'm pretty sure."

Tully heard a sound at the door and spun around. Vera was standing there with Susan. "Oh, my goodness!" she gasped. "I am just so glad you let me come along. Thank you, Bo, thank you! This is my first crime scene ever!"

"No problem," Tully said. He thought maybe he should hire Vera for the department. Most of his deputies were wimps. It might be good to have someone in the department who was actually bloodthirsty.

Chapter 15

Bo spent the rest of the weekend sleeping at his house. Monday noon he stumbled into the office. As he walked across the briefing room, Daisy smiled at him. "You've got a visitor, boss. She nodded toward the glassed-in wall of his office. A gray-haired lady sat in one of his chairs. She had very good posture, her back straight as an arrow, all business. Jan Whittle! Principal of the Delmore Blight Grade School and Middle School. With the downturn in the economy, the middle school had been added to her duties as principal. He and Jan had been boyfriend and girlfriend in sixth grade. As far as he could recall, they had never spoken even once in sixth grade, but that was the way of sixth-grade romance back then. She had grown into a stern but interesting woman. Too bad she was still married to Darrel Whittle, the oaf of a district attorney, because he wouldn't mind dating her. This time they might even talk. He had no trouble guessing what had brought her to his office.

Opening the door he growled, “No, Jan, absolutely not!”

She turned to glare at him. “You most certainly will, Bo! You're sheriff of Blight County!”

He slid into his chair. “Every fall Glenn Cliff runs off to the mountains, and I have to hunt him down. Last fall I found him holed up in an abandoned logging camp. He'll know better than to go there again. “He's probably built himself a wickiup somewhere even deeper in the mountains this time.”

“Bo, he's just a kid. He'll die up there. The snow will trap him on some mountain and he won't be able to get out.”

“What's your point, Jan?” he said, earning himself another glare. He studied her, pretending to think about the Cliff boy. She was very nice looking, in a fit and serious sort of way. On the other hand, he was a year older. So was Glen, about thirteen now. The kid spent summers stashing away food and gear up in the mountains, preparing for his yearly getaway in the fall, his escape from school, which bored him nearly to death. This would be Tully's third year of tracking him down. The thought made him shudder.

Jan took a handkerchief out of her purse and dabbed at her eyes.

“Don't cry, Jan. I'll go find the little . . .”

“I wasn't crying, Bo! I just had something in my eye!”

Ah,the old something-in-my-eye ploy. “I only happen to have a bank robbery and five murders to tend with at the moment, so I'll drop everything and go hunt Glen Cliff. But this is absolutely the last time, Jan!"

She smiled. "You say that every year, Bo."

"I guess I do. This year though, you have to buy me dinner at Crabbs. That's if I find Glen, of course."

"Bo, I would love to buy you dinner anywhere you name! And any time!"

"How about the Space Needle in Seattle?"

She thought for a moment. "That sounds more like a proposition."

"I meant it to. How are you and old Darrel getting along these days?"

"Fine, now that we've decided to get a divorce."

Tully tugged on the corner of his mustache. "That usually helps. You still living together?"

"You're awfully inquisitive."

"That's part of a sheriff's job."

Jan laughed, then turned serious. "Do you have any idea where Glen might be?"

"Not the foggiest. We have about ten thousand square miles of mountains in Blight County and he could be hiding out on any of them. But it so happens I ran into him this summer fishing up on Boulder Creek, which as you probably know comes tumbling down out of the mountains north of town. It levels off a couple of miles up the creek and there's a nice meadow there. If I were to run away to the mountains, I think I'd head for the meadow on Boulder Creek."

"You thought about doing this when you were Glen's age?"

"Then and now."

Jan smoothed her skirt over her rather nice thighs. "So if you were to take off this minute, Bo, you would head for that meadow?"

He was silent for a few moments. Jan said, "Bo?"

"Sorry. I was just building my self a nice little wick-iup on the edge of the meadow. I'd fish the creek and hunt game for food. There's gold in the creek, too. If I had time I might even find the mother lode. It would be a lovely way to live, Jan? You interested?"

"I'll have to think about that, Bo. No!" Jan smiled. "So when do you think you will head off to look for Glen."

Tully stared at her, then laughed. "As soon as I can catch the next flight to Boulder Creek."

"You're hopeless, Bo!"

"I know, but I mean it about the flight."

After Jan left, he walked to the door. "Daisy, see if you can find the number for the Diamond W logging-truck dispatcher and ask him to patch me through to Pete Reynolds."

Daisy smiled and shook her head. "I guess Pete can't escape you even when he's out driving loads of logs down a mountain."

"No one escapes me, Daisy, any time or any place. You know that."

He walked over to Lurch's corner. "You get any matches on the bullets that did Beeker and Dance."

"Yeah. They match the forty-five we picked up from Shanks. Susan sent me the bullets recovered from the old couple, too, boss."

"Great, Lurch! I figured she would."

"Yeah, but they don't match either pistol found with Beeker and Dance. Maybe they dumped that gun somewhere. The rifle that killed Vergil Stone belonged to Beeker. He was the shooter on Chimney Rock Mountain. At least the rifle that has his prints on it is the same one that shot Vergil. The test slug matches the bullet recovered from the vic's body."

Tully nodded and pulled up a chair next to the Unit. "Shut down your computer a minute, and I'll give you benefit of my profound thought processes."

Lurch shut off his computer.

Tully clasped his hands behind his head and leaned back in his chair. "First of all, the old lady in the double-wide was either a Beeker or a descendent of Beekers. She might have known Horace Beeker as some kind of family relation. I suspect most of the Beekers had fallen on hard times since losing the ranch or whatever happened that Beekers no longer own it. The old lady might have suspected that Horace Beeker was hiding out from something or someone. I've got Daisy checking with the corporation that owns the ranch. Somebody will know what the old people were doing there, watching over the mansion or whatever. Maybe Beeker didn't want the woman to identify him and give him up to whoever might be looking for him. So he killed her and the old man just to be on the safe side. Beeker and Dance, of course, didn't want Harold or Alma giving away their hideout, so that, too, could be the motive for killing them. If they needed a motive."

Lurch nodded. "Sounds about right. I guess if you get started killing, another one more or less doesn't bother you all that much."

Tully stared at him. "That's why you don't get to carry a gun, Lurch."

"I thought it was because of my eyes."

"That too. My opinion is that the main reason Beeker or Dance shot them, hardly anyone knew about the lookout tower on Round Top, and he wanted to keep it that way. The tower made the perfect hideout. They could hang out there until the search for them let up."

Lurch frowned. "If it was so perfect, how come Beeker and Dance ended up dead?"

"Details, Lurch, details. I'm pretty sure I know who shot them. All we need is some proof."

"I think we have the proof, boss. The bullets that killed Beeker and Dance match the test bullets I got from one of the pistols you picked up from Shanks."

Tully nodded. "That's great, Lurch! So we can nail him for two murders, even though he'll probably plead self-defense."

"I thought so. You going to let me carry a gun now?"

"No." Tully stared off into space.

"What are you thinking, boss?"

"I'm starting to think converging incidentals aren't merely incidentals. As a matter of fact, I'm headed out to Shanks's place right now."

Lurch got up to leave. "You going to arrest him?"

"Yeah, I'm going to arrest him."

"On what charge? Murder?"

"Yes, murder. A double murder. And a convergence."

Lurch gave him a puzzled look. "A convergence of what, boss?"

"Beats the heck out of me. Just a convergence, Lurch. Maybe a convergence of fingers, all of them are pointing at Gridley Shanks. This all started with the partial fingerprint you turned up on a piece of flagging tape. To explain the flagging tape, Grid said he used it to mark his property so two men could hunt elk there.

One of them was Beeker, who said he saw a herd of deer that came through hours before he claimed to be on the mountain. Then the Beeker name led us to the Beeker Ranch and four murdered people, including Beeker and Dance. Then . . ."

"Stop, boss! I get the idea! What did you call it?"

"A convergence. Lines of suspicion that all converge on Gridley Shanks."

Lurch shook his head. "Too complicated for me, boss."

"Well, I'm headed out to Shanks place right now to arrest him on suspicion of murdering Beeker and Dance."

Chapter 16

The road leading into Shanks's house was still bright yellow with fallen needles from the tamarack trees. Tully almost hated to drive on it, as if he were somehow desecrating a work of literature. He blinked. Danielle Stone was standing in front of the house, watching him. What was she doing here?

"Danielle!" he exclaimed as he stepped out of the Explorer.

"Hi, Sheriff. I'm here exploring my new property."

"I don't understand."

She laughed. "I don't understand either. Grid had his lawyer draw up some legal papers that made the property mine. Believe me, Sheriff, it's not that great a gift. I was trying to figure out what I can get when I sell it. Not that much, I'm afraid."

Tully look around. "So where are Grid and Sil going to live?"

"I don't know. Maybe Grid will figure that out when he gets back."

Tully glanced into the woodshed. The ATV was still there. "Get back from where?"

"Beats the heck out of me. He packed up Sil, and she took off on a trip around the world. She should be in Australia by now. Grid's been talking about a round-the-world trip for years, but I never thought he was serious. He should have sent me with her."

Tully thought about this. After a bit he said, "Yeah, he should have found a way to include his own daughter."

Danielle frowned at him. "Daughter! What do you mean, *daughter*? That's sick! Grid has been my lover for the past five years. No way I'm his daughter. I know exactly who my parents are!"

Tully leaned against the hood of his Explorer. He had known Grid was a confidence man and a good one, he just hadn't realized how good. He must have come into a fair amount of money recently, sending Sil on a round-the-world trip. Giving his place to Danielle. More lines of convergence. Who ends up with the loot? Who has a motive for killing Beeker and Dance?

Danielle said, "Yeah, Grid's been supporting me and Vergil for years. He brought us groceries and more fruit and vegetables than we could ever eat. I tell you, Sheriff, I'll never eat another banana as long as I live. And he kept Vergil supplied with cash. Said he was starting to think of him as his own son, not that he seemed all that upset when Vergil got killed."

Tully studied the widow Stone. She looked as if she were perfectly capable of taking care of herself.

"Listen, Danielle, if you need any help, just give me a call, okay?"

She eyed him thoughtfully. "You bet, Sheriff. By the way, my friends call me Danny."

"Danny. I like that."

Another piece of the Gridley puzzle had fallen into place. There's a bank robbery. Three of the robbers are eventually killed. The loot disappears. Grid suddenly has enough money to send Sil on a round-the-world trip. "By the way, Danielle, do you have any idea how Gridley suddenly came into enough money to pay for a trip around the world?"

She laughed. "Sure. He's rich. He owned houses in town, farms out in the country, all kinds of ranch and grazing land. He sold most of it over the last year. He's at least a millionaire, probably several times over."

Tully thought about the bank job. He knew places in the world where a person could live in luxury forever just on the money from the bank. He didn't know exactly how much money that was, but enough almost to fill a trash bag.

Danielle said, "Maybe after I unload Grid's stupid place, I'll move to Boise. At least its got some great restaurants."

"Yes, it does."

"Oh, by the way. Grid told me to give you the ATV. So it's yours, whenever you want to pick it up."

Tully stood there, stunned by this announcement. What if Lurch matched the ATV track on the mountain to Grid's machine? He suspected a sinister joke by its absentee owner. This would take some thought. "By the way, Danny, do you have any idea where Grid might be right now? Did he ever mention a particular country he might head for?"

She thought for a moment. "Well, he talked a lot about Australia and all the different birds there. He has a thing about birds, I don't know why. I personally think birds are about as boring as it gets, but for some reason Grid is crazy about them."

Tully scratched his jaw and stared off into the distance. "So right now, Danny, you think Grid may at this very moment be on a plane headed to Australia?"

"This very moment? Naw. At this very moment he's eating lunch at Slade's. After that he's driving his Caddy to Arkansas. You ever heard of something called an ivory-billed woodpecker?"

"I have. Thank you very much, Danny. I'll see if I can catch up with Grid at Slade's. In regard to the ATV, I couldn't personally accept it. The whole county would interpret it as graft. On the other hand, if it were used in commission of a crime, the department could confiscate it as evidence. But thanks for the offer."

Slade's was relatively quiet. A group of the usual unemployed were shooting pool in the back. Joey was minding the bar. Shanks was sitting at a table by himself, munching a hamburger with fries. Tully pulled out a chair and sat down across from him.

"Why, hi, Bo," Shanks said. "What brings you to Slade's this time of day?"

Tully said, "Let me think a minute. Oh, it's you I was looking for, Grid. I might be here to arrest you."

"Arrest me? For what? You got any kind of evidence I committed a crime, Sheriff?"

"Grid, it's Blight County. I don't need evidence. It's simpler if I do, of course."

Shanks laughed. "You know me, Bo. I'm always

happy to help out the law when I can."

"Well, let's see. There's the matter of two killings up at Round Top lookout. The victims were shot with a gun we've tied to you."

Shanks smiled. "That's probably a gun I sold to a fellow passing through. He shot somebody in a lookout, you say? I have no idea who it could have been. Maybe he was in on the bank robbery with Dance and Beeker. I assume the reason you hunted me down, you found my fingerprints at the scene of the crime."

"No, we didn't turn up any fingerprints belonging to you, Grid. We also didn't find a large garbage bag stuffed with loot from a bank robbery."

"Okay, Sheriff, suppose I shot Beeker and Dance. I would have shot them in self-defense. I'm sure Beeker and Dance must have been armed."

"Yeah, we saw that. We also noticed the loot had disappeared."

Shanks picked up a french fry and munched it. "You don't think I'd still be sitting around here if I had picked up the loot, do you, Bo? By the way, if I killed them, it would have been because they killed the old couple. I couldn't think of any reason they wanted to kill them, except maybe to conceal their track to the lookout or the fact the lookout even existed. I was furious with them for killing the old lady and her husband, but mostly because the loot had disappeared. I figured the reason they killed Harold and Alma, was to to keep them quiet about something they saw. Say, I have to hit the john. You mind?"

"Give me your word you won't try to split out the back, because I don't escort men to the restroom."

"You're so easy, Bo. Yeah, you have my word. Besides

here comes the FBI." Shanks got up and walked into the restroom. Angie stopped and glowered down at Tully.

"Sheriff, you just let Gridley Shanks walk into the restroom by himself! He's my main suspect, and he could be a block away by now!" She pulled a gun from her shoulder bag and charged into the restroom.

A man inside yelled, "Whoa! Lady! Watch it with the gun! I ain't the one what done it, whatever it is!"

A large man with a gray beard and mustache charged out of the restroom, looking back over his shoulder. A few seconds later, Angie came out tugging Grid by the front flap of his jacket, her gun in the other hand.

Her lips quivering with rage, she said, "I can't understand you, Bo, letting a man we know committed two murders disappear into a restroom by himself!"

"It's the Blight way," Tully said. "I don't accompany men to the restroom, Angie. That's all. And he gave me his word he wouldn't break and run. Besides, the windows in there are way too small for him to wiggle through."

Angie shoved Shanks into a chair and sat down next to him. She put her gun away but didn't zip the shoulder bag.

Shanks said to Tully, "I hope you don't mind the wet stain I have running down my pant leg."

"Not at all," Tully said. "I practically have one myself."

Shanks said, "Anyway, those window are so dirty I couldn't bring myself to touch one of them."

"Yeah, Grid, I figured that would also be the case. So let's hear your theory about the murder of the old couple."

Shanks sighed and leaned back in his chair. "I'd been trying to track down Beeker and Dance and went to the library to see if I could find a map of the area around Famine. A little old lady came over to help and told me she had written a history book on Blight County. We got to talking and she told me about the Beeker Ranch and the annual picnics Beeker threw on Round Top and the lookout up there. I started putting two and two together."

Angie gave Tully a hard look. "I had to find out from Daisy you were over here interrogating a murder and bank-robbery suspect."

"Well, I was thinking of Grid here more as a double-murder suspect. We know he killed Beeker and Dance."

She shook her head. "Can I be satisfied that he will be safely confined in the Blight County jail for tonight?"

"By all means."

Angie got up and left.

Shanks shoved what was left of his fries out into the middle of the table. "Help yourself, Bo."

"No thanks. I've eaten here before."

"I know what you mean. So, you want to hear my theory about the murder of the old couple?"

"Shoot."

"Well, killing them seemed a bit extreme even for Beeker and Dance. I couldn't think of any reason to shoot them, except just out of meanness. They probably tossed the guns in the river, so I doubt you can prove they killed them either."

"You're pretty sure Dance and Beeker killed them?"

"Yeah. You think I killed Beeker and Dance and took the loot. Well, the loot wasn't there. If it had been, I wouldn't be sitting here talking to you."

"It wasn't there?"

"No. If it had been, right now I'd be hanging out with Sil in some ritzy hotel in Australia."

"So why aren't you?"

"Because I don't have the loot! Here's what I think happened. You want to hear?"

"Go ahead."

"They didn't want the loot to be found with them, so they hid it."

"Where?"

"I don't know."

"It's in the old Beeker mansion, isn't it?"

Shanks rolled his eyes. "Why I let myself get drawn into conversations with you I have no idea. But, yes, I think that's where the money is. But that's only a guess. I think Harold and Alma saw either Beeker or Dance carry a bundle into the mansion and come back without it. They may have been old, but the bank robbery was all over the radio, and they wouldn't have to think too hard about what was in the bag. Why does someone hide something in a burnt-out old mansion? The old couple weren't stupid. So Beeker or Dance sees them watching out a window and walks over and shoots them."

Tully glanced at his watch. "You want to go for a ride right now, Grid?"

"We split the loot fifty-fifty, if we find it?"

"You sound like my father. But the answer is no. If we find the loot and return it to the bank, it may do you some good in front of a jury, but I can't promise anything." He took out his phone and dialed Angie.

"What, Bo?"

"How would you like to take a ride out to the old Beeker mansion?"

"Now?"

"Yeah. Maybe to find the bank loot and solve the murder of the old couple."

Angie was silent, apparently turning all this over in her mind. "This doesn't have anything to do with the Blight way, does it, Bo?"

"The Blight way? What's that? Grid and I will pick you up in twenty minutes at your hotel. I've got to stop by the office first."

"Okay, but we take Pap and the tracker along. I don't trust either you or Grid as far as I can throw you."

"I doubt Dave can make it, but I'll give him a call."

He stopped by the office and called Pap from there. He told the old man to get himself armed and that he and Angie would be pick him up in half an hour.

"What's up, Bo?"

"You, Angie and I are going on a treasure hunt with Gridley Shanks."

"What about Dave?"

"For heavens sake, Pap, don't you think we can handle one measly desperado without the tracker?"

Pap was silent for a moment. Then he said, "I guess that way we can split the loot four ways instead of five. What are you waiting for, Bo? Let's go!"

Tully walked down to the garage. He had left Shanks handcuffed to the steering wheel of the Explorer. Unlocking the cuff, he said, "You make a run for it, Grid, I'll shoot you dead."

Shanks frowned. "That seems terribly rude, Bo. I can assure you I have no intention of making a run for it, at least until we find the loot."

The sun went behind a cloud just as they arrived at the mansion, giving the burnt-out structure an even more ominous look. Tully was reminded of the dark threat Etta had sensed hovering around him. He wondered if it had anything to do with Shanks. He said, "Grid, I hope this treasure hunt isn't some ruse you thought up so you could slip away into the mountains."

Shanks said, "What I know is, I didn't find the loot with Beeker and Dance at the tower. I killed them because they tried to kill me. Self defense. Also for them killing Harold and Alma. I couldn't think of any reason for them to kill an old couple like that, except for pure meanness or to keep them quiet about the lookout. But now my guess is they saw Beeker and Dance haul something into the mansion and come back without it. Maybe one of them saw Harold or Alma staring out the window, so he killed them, just to be on the safe side. All we have to do is find the hiding place, and we've got the bag of loot."

Tully said, "You make it sound easy, Grid."

"I didn't mean to."

"There are a lot of hiding places in that old building," Angie said. "We'll probably get killed trying to find them."

Tully stared up at the mansion. The structure was even creepier than he remembered. The four of them walked over to the entrance and peered in.

The inside of the mansion was in a greater state of ruin than Tully had even guessed.

Shanks said, "Be careful where you step or you could find yourself zooming down through a floor or two. Everything that's not burnt is rotten from one end to the other. The staircase looks like it's in halfway decent shape, so Pap and I will work our way up to the second floor. You and Angie take the first floor."

Pap scratched his chin as he stared up the blackened staircase. "Looks haunted to me, Grid. Worse, the timbers that ain't burned through are rotted. If we see a ghost, I doubt any of them would give me traction."

Grid laughed as they started up the stairs. "Walk on the edge of the steps, Pap. You step in the middle of them, you may take an express elevator into the basement."

Tully watched them make their way to the second floor and disappear into the darkness of a vast room off to one side.

While Pap and Shanks searched the second floor, Tully and Angie searched the first, the beams of their flashlights seeming to disappear into the blackened walls. As they worked their way into what might once have been a nursery, Pap shouted down to them.

"Bo! We just found the piano Richy and I heard when we canoed down the river! It's huge!"

Tully turned to Angie. "I still suspect the piano music they heard came from the caretakers' trailer house."

Angie laughed. "I still prefer the idea of a ghost playing a ghost piano."

Suddenly, they heard a great crash from upstairs. The whole mansion seemed to moan.

"What now?" Tully yelled, suspecting that Pap and Shanks were now back on the first floor.

There was a long moment of silence upstairs. Then Pap yelled down, "Grid just lifted the lid off the piano and threw it on the floor."

Tully shouted at them. "You two are making me a nervous wreck! Don't lift anything more! Come back downstairs!"

Angie said, "Bo, I just found the door to the cellar. That would be a great place to hide the loot."

Tully walked over and looked down the steps. The walls on both sides were draped with spider webs. Ugly smells drifted up.

Tully sniffed. "If the loot is down there, it will have to stay there, unless you want to go down and prowl around, Angie."

She swept the beam of her flashlight across the floor. "I would, but it looks like at least a foot of water down there."

"I think I see something swimming in it," Tully said. He walked over to a room that must have been a library. Lining the walls were dozens of shelves, some of which contained blackened blobs of things that must once have been books.

"This is a surprise," he said. "Old Beeker must have been quite the literate fellow, particularly for Blight County." He picked a copy off a shelf and opened it to see if he could read the title. The book collapsed in his hand. "Well, I've had enough of this."

He and Angie worked their way slowly through two other large rooms. In the last one, the floor under Tully started to collapse and Angie jerked him back to safety. "That's enough of this," he said. "If the loot is here, the ghosts can have it." They walked back to the entryway.

"Hey, Pap!" he called. "Let's get out of here, before the place collapses on one of us."

No answer.

"Pap! Grid!"

Still no answer.

He heard a noise at the top of the stairs. Pap was standing there, rubbing the back of his head. He took a tentative step down the stairs and seemed about to fall. Tully rushed up the steps and grabbed him.

"Grid hit me in the back of my head with something. Knocked me cold. I saw him head for the stairs. He wasn't carrying anything but I think he may have tossed something out a window. I was looking inside the piano when something whacked me on the back of the head."

"You okay, Pap?"

"Yeah, just help me down the stairs. I think Shanks tossed the bag of loot out the window. Go get him, Bo!"

"I intend to do just that."

Angie came up the stairs and put her arm around Pap. "I've got him, Bo. Go get Shanks."

Tully started down the stairs.

"One thing, Bo!" Pap called after him.

"What's that?"

"He took my gun!"

Tully felt himself sag. He stepped out on to the porch. No sign of Shanks. It would have been easy for him to make it to the woods. He took out his gun and fired two shots in the air.

"What was that for?" Angie said. "To warn him he'd better come back?"

"Yeah," Tully said. "I'm done fooling around with Gridley Shanks."

He came back and helped Pap to the Explorer and inserted him into the back seat of the Explorer. He grabbed a bottle of water out of the luggage area and handed it to the old man.

"Stop fussing with me, Bo! Go get him! He's got the loot!"

Tully rushed back to the front of the mansion. Angie was standing there, her gun out. "This reeks of the Blight way, Bo!"

Tully stared at the woods. Then they heard a shot. They looked at each other. "I think he shot himself," Angie said. "Maybe he figured there was no way out."

"I hate this job," Tully said.

Angie shook her head. "We should go look for the body."

"I suppose," Tully said.

They crisscrossed back and forth through the woods for an hour. Finally, he found Angie, her gun hanging limply from one hand, her forehead resting against a tamarack. The needles had drifted down and turned her hair a bright yellow.

She straightened up when she heard Tully. "Couldn't find the body?" she said.

"A bear must have dragged it off."

"Bears are hibernating by now," she said.

"In that case, wolves. A pack of wolves could have dragged it off."

Angie sighed. "Strange how fast a person becomes an it."

"Yeah."

Just then the quavering howl of a wolf came drifting through the woods."

"See what I told you," Tully said. "A wolf got him. We may as well head in."

"You're giving up, Bo?"

"Yeah, we'll let the wolves have Shanks."

They headed back toward Famine, each of them absorbed in thoughts they didn't care to share. Pap sat in back smoking one of his handrolleds. Tully didn't even bother to yell at him.

As they approached the intersection of Beeker Road and the Old River Road, Angie pointed up ahead. Pap straightened up and peered out the windshield. "That looks like Dave's big, old, white truck."

"It does, all right," Tully said. "Wonder what brought him out here?"

Tully pulled up alongside the pickup and stopped. The tracker had his arm resting in the open window. Gridley Shanks sat next him, his right arm above his head and handcuffed to a door strap.

Angie rolled down her window. "Dave, you caught him! How on earth did you show up here?"

"You don't think Bo would venture out with a dangerous criminal like Shanks here without a backup, do you, Angie."

She shook her head. "I guess not."

Tully said, "I thought that wolfs howl was a little shaky, Dave."

"When the wolf has to chase an escaped criminal up the side of a mountain, his howl deserves to be shaky. Just as he got to the old foot bridge, he took a shot at me. I should have had you fire three shots: two if unarmed, three, if he has a gun. The gun slowed me up a little."

Angie said, "Oh! That wolf's howl! It was the signal you had caught him!"

"Yep. It wasn't the first time we've used that signal, right, Bo?"

"Right, but it may be the last. Say, Angie, you want to ride into Famine with Dave?"

"You don't mind, Bo?" Angie said.

"Naw. I'll trade you for Grid."

"You're awful easy, Bo," the tracker said.

"Yeah," Tully said. "I must be getting old. You get the loot, Dave?"

"I got a black trash bag full of something that feels like money. I didn't look!"

Pap said, "Maybe you should let me look after it, Dave. That much money can be awfully tempting."

"Yeah, I know, Pap. I'll lock it up in my safe for the night. How does that sound to you, Bo?"

"That's what I would do. I'll arrange for the FBI to pick it up tomorrow. How does that sound, Angie?"

"It sounds a lot like the Blight way, but I'm so tired even that is starting to sound good to me."

Chapter 17

The next morning, Daisy followed Tully into his office. He flopped into his chair and put his boots up on the desk, his hands clasped behind his head. "I'm beginning to hate roughing it in the wilds," he said. "So, what's happening here?"

"Your friendly FBI agent wants you to call her. She's at the bank and says they're about to wrap up their investigation."

"She give you her cell number? I had it, but probably threw it away."

"I bet," Daisy said. "But I'll get it for you."

"Send in Lurch, please."

"Hey, Byron, the boss wants you!" she shouted across the briefing room to the Unit.

Tully sighed. "I could have shouted at him from here, Daisy."

She came back and handed Tully a slip of paper with Angie's number on it. "It's just that I know you're tired, Bo."

Lurch stopped in the doorway. Daisy squeezed past him on her way out.

Tully smiled. "I guess that's the highlight of your day, Lurch."

"More like my month. Would you mind calling Daisy back in when I start to leave?"

"Afraid not. Two squeezes like that in one day could kill even a young fellow like you. So, what do we have on the murder of the old couple."

Lurch pulled up a chair and sat down across the desk.

Tully stared at him over the pointed toes of his boots. "So, did you get around to checking the bullets that killed the old couple? I suppose you've already checked Beeker and Dance's handguns."

"Yeah, but there seems to be a gun missing. The guns found with Beekeer and Dance didn't kill Alma and Harold. Still working on it, boss. I've been looking over a bunch of stuff my predecessor left in the store-room. Pretty interesting, and . . ."

"Lurch, you're supposed to be working, not entertaining yourself."

"I am working, boss. My job is a whole lot more complicated than you think."

"Yeah, yeah."

"Part of it is somebody keeps piling work on me, not to mention any names."

"Yes, I know, somebody gives you so much work you hardly have time for your computer games. I'll have to speak to that person when I get a chance. You made casts of the tire tracks at the lookout, right?"

"Right. One set belongs to an old pickup belonging to one Shanks, as you suspected. It's got a couple of hay bales in the bed, apparently to weigh down the rear end for traction. At least we can show the truck was at the scene of the shooting of Dance and Beeker. There were no other tracks there except from our vehicles and the Land Rover, which was registered to Beeker. "

Tully said, "That should tie Shanks to the lookout about the time of the shooting of Beeker and Dance. He has already admitted to killing them, but it never hurts to have a little extra evidence. Still, he might get off on his claim of self defense."

Lurch got up to leave. "If you run into the person causing me all this work, I hope you speak harshly to him."

"Yeah, yeah, you can count on that, Lurch." Tully spun around in his chair to look out his window at Lake Blight. Snow had already capped the high mountains on the far side. It was going to be another hard winter. There had been a time when he loved hard winters, but not anymore.

Tully spun back around. "Hey, Lurch, the bullet that killed Vergil. You get a match for it?"

Lurch stopped in the doorway. "Yeah, I thought I already told you. It matches a test bullet from Beeker's rifle, at least a seven-millimeter rifle with his prints on it."

"Great. I figured he was the one that shot Vergil, but I like to clean up any loose ends. We now know that Beeker was on Chimney Rock Mountain at least three hours before the shooting."

Lurch blinked. "We do?"

"Yeah, the weather girl at the TV station checked the time of the snowfall for me."

"She can do that?"

"Yeah, so we know the exact time the deer herd went through, the herd Beeker claims to have seen, because the tracks were half filled with fresh snow. So that puts him at the scene nearly four hours before the murder and three hours before he claims to have been there. He never saw the herd of elk come over the same trail, because by then he was up in the woods waiting for Vergil."

Lurch waited in the doorway, apparently hoping for another squeeze from Daisy. He said, "Even if we show Shanks's ATV was at the scene the time of Vergil Stone's murder, that doesn't prove Shanks was there."

"Details, Lurch, details."

Lurch rubbed his forehead. "Do I need a warrant to make casts of Shanks's ATV tires?"

"No, because Shanks has given the department his ATV. So find a trailer, and you and Thorpe go pick it up."

Tully took out his pocket notebook, wrote in it and tore out the page. "Here's Shanks's address. Just to be on the safe side, swing by Judge Patterson's office and pick up a search warrant."

Lurch stared at the slip of paper. "What's going on, Bo? Patterson usually gives you a warrant after you find what you're looking for."

"Yeah, but this time we'd better go by the book."

"Which book is that?"

"Beats the heck out of me. I haven't seen it around here in years. But we'd better go by it, anyway. On your way out, send Daisy in here."

"Right, boss."

"No, Lurch! Not while you're standing in the doorway. You've already had your squeeze for the day."

Lurch went off muttering, and Daisy soon popped in the door, her stenographer's book in hand.

"What's wrong with Lurch, Bo?"

"The usual. Just being Lurch is a full-time job. I was wondering if you would like to join me for a celebration dinner at Crabbs this evening.

"What are we celebrating?"

"That remains to be seen."

Daisy stared at him. "What else did you have in mind?"

"Eating. Unless you have a better suggestion."

She smiled. "Eating sounds pretty good to me. Eating and drinking sounds even better."

"The drinking goes without saying. It's a date then. I'll pick you up at your desk after work."

Chapter 18

Lester was obviously pleased to see Tully back with Daisy. He seated them at their special table, up near the front of the dining room. While they waited for their martinis, another waiter brought them a plate of raw vegetables and dips. "Compliments of Lester," he said.

They had ordered vodka martinis. Upon his return with the drinks, Lester stood by awaiting the couple's approval. Tully sipped his and glanced up at Lester. "There's something wrong with this martini, Lester."

Lester looked horrified. "What?"

"I can taste actual vodka in it."

"Me too!" Daisy said.

Lester smiled. "That's because I made them myself. The vodka is top of the line. And I added an extra dollop. I figured if I got the two of you drunk, I might get you back together."

"Good thinking, Lester, "Daisy said, laughing. "Two sips and Bo is already starting to looked pretty good to me. I may require a couple more of these martinis, though."

Lester disappeared into the kitchen, smiling broadly.

Daisy sipped her martini again. "So, Bo, fill me in on our murders."

That was one of the things he liked about dating Daisy. They could always talk business. He munched a piece of celery, took another swig of his martini and blinked a couple of times. He tried to clear his throat, but his voice had already become gravelly. "What we have here, Daisy, is a convergence. It may seem like a simple bank robbery, but it's actually a convergence."

She peered at him over the top of her martini glass. "What's a convergence?"

"It's where certain things start coming together. Or seem to. For example, lines of suspicion start emanating from various situations and clues and they converge on a particular point."

"And that point is?"

"Gridley Shanks."

"And who provided you with this theory?"

"Gridley Shanks."

Daisy set down her martini and frowned. "Why would Shanks give you a theory that pointed to him as a killer and robber?"

"Grid's point exactly. He said usually a convergence is only a convergence and has no meaning. That's what he claimed after I told him about some of the evidence pointing to him. He said a convergence gives you a false conclusion."

"Describe this convergence."

"The partial fingerprint Lurch found on the strip of flagging tape that happened to be hanging from a limb right at the point Vergil drove the getaway car into the ditch. The Unit matched the partial print on the tape to Grid."

Daisy shook her head. "That tape is ubiquitous."

"Yeah, I know, and besides that, it's everywhere. But I had to ask myself, how do you tie a piece of flagging tape to a branch and not leave more than a partial fingerprint on it. I figured you had to wipe the tape. But why wipe flagging tape except to get rid of your fingerprints?"

"Maybe the prints belonged to an extremely neat person?"

Tully frowned. "I don't think so, Daisy. Anyway, I hunted Shanks down at his home, and he was very cooperative, even agreed to introduce me to the two fellows who wanted to hunt his land, the two guys who, to hear them tell it, arrived at the scene of the shooting about the same time it occurred. Grid put up the tape, presumably, to show them where to hunt. Anyway, according to Grid, that explained the tape's hanging from the tree, and the two hunters would vouch for the fact it served no other purpose than to show them the property owned by Grid."

"And did they?"

"Did they what?"

"I've forgotten. You know something, Bo? This is the best martini I've had in years."

"I believe it. But, yes, I think these two guys had been properly schooled by Grid. They said all the right things, except one of them mentioned seeing a herd of deer."

Daisy stood up and waved her hand. "Lester, we're going to need another round of martinis here pretty quick! I'm caught in a convergence!"

Tully frowned at her. "Very funny. Do you want to hear this or not?"

"Yes, I really do." She sat back down. "It's just that martinis help me focus my attention."

"I bet."

Daisy picked up a radish, dipped it in salt and thoughtfully munched it. "Any more to this convergence?"

"Yes, indeed. It turns out that the victim, Vergil Stone, was the husband of Grid's mistress. The night after Vergil's murder I found Grid's car parked in Vergil's garage. When I mentioned this to Grid he explained he was sitting up with the widow because she was his daughter, the result of an affair many years ago. I later mentioned this to the young lady. She scoffed at this bit of information. She said no way was she Grid's daughter. She had been his lover ever since she had got out of high school. The Stones were getting a divorce. Among other things, Vergil's getting murdered saved the cost of the divorce. Grid was always looking to the upside of things."

Daisy dropped a carrot stick halfway to her mouth. "What! She told you that?"

"No, I reached that conclusion myself. I don't think the widow Stone was involved in Vergil's murder, but Grid owned their house and had been supplying the couple with money. He probably saw the murder as an inexpensive divorce, but the main reason was to shut up a weak link in the bank robbery and cut Vergil out of his share of the loot."

Lester delivered them each a second martini and asked if they were ready to order.

Tully stared at him blankly. "What?"

"Food," Lester said. "When folks dine at Crabbs sooner or later they like to order food, unless of course they've heard some of the unfounded rumors."

Tully and Daisy each went with the wood-fired shrimp, even though both doubted the authenticity of a wood fire. After Lester had left and stopped by another table to chat with the diners, Daisy said, "So what happened to the loot?"

Tully shoved his second martini away from him. "Here's my theory. I vaguely recall going by an old pickup truck headed into town when we were in pursuit of the getaway vehicle. I suspect it was parked alongside the road between town and the point Vergil ran the getaway car into the ditch. I supposed the driver had pulled over to the side of the road to avoid our pursuit vehicles. The driver of the truck I took to be a farmer— striped overalls, battered hat pulled low over the eyes, tattered jacket, the usual outfit for one of our farmers. There were a couple of hay bales in the back of the truck. So let's say Vergil slid to a stop, Dance jumped out of the getaway car with the loot, dove with it into the bed of the pickup, and pulled a tarp over him. The fourth guy in the robbery drives the pickup off toward town as soon as we pass him."

Daisy sipped her martini. "So who's driving the pickup, if Dance dived into the back of it with the loot, with Beeker waiting up on the mountain to shoot Vergil?"

"The fourth guy—Gridley Shanks."

"Yeah." Tully tugged on the corner of his mustache while he thought about this. "We're pretty sure the actual robber was Dance. Vergil's job was to keep the getaway car running."

Daisy stared at him. "So Shanks was involved in the robbery?"

"Yes. More than that. My guess is he's also the mastermind of the whole thing. We even found a pickup truck parked out in his woods. It looks a good deal like the pickup I saw on the Canyon Creek road."

Lester arrived with two salads. He set a bowl of dressing next to each. "Blue cheese dressing on the side for both, if I recall correctly."

"You're terrific, Lester!" Daisy said.

"Thank you, my dear. The wood-grilled shrimp will be out in a moment. May I bring you each another martini?"

Tully looked up at him. "That depends on whether you have a free taxi service to haul soused diners home."

"Would that be two residences or one, sir?"

Tully looked at Daisy. She smiled back.

"That remains to be seen, Lester, but for now, hold off on martinis for me."

Daisy forked out some salad, dipped it in her blue-cheese dressing, and poked it in her mouth, missing on the first thrust, but connecting on the second.

After dinner, Tully drove Daisy to her home, carried her into her bedroom, poured her into bed, kissed her on the forehead, and started toward the door.

"I really needed that, Bo."

"The kiss?"

"No, the martinis."

The last was part whisper, part doze.

As he was climbing into the Explorer his cell phone rang. He pulled it out and looked at it. Lurch! "What are you calling me for at this hour? Can't you sleep?"

"Sleep? What's that, boss?"

"You're still at work?"

"Yeah. I just put together something I thought you'd be interested in."

"Well, since it won't wait until morning, shoot."

"You remember that hassle Shanks got into with those bikers at Slade's."

"Yeah."

"He was carrying a concealed weapon. He had a permit for it but when he was arrested, his weapon was confiscated. Before returning it, my predecessor ran a ballistics check on it to see if it had been used in any crimes. He didn't find any, but he kept the bullet and all the paper work. I just checked the bullet against the bullets that killed the old couple. They were a match."

"Shanks killed them? Then it must have been Shanks that Alma and Harold saw walking into the Beeker mansion with the loot! That was why he had to kill them! He substituted the dead Beeker and Dance for himself. Good work, Lurch!"

'"So, can I take the day off tomorrow, boss?"

Tully checked his watch. It was almost 1:00 in the morning. "Let me think about that. Well, okay, Lurch, but don't let this get to be a habit."

The next morning Tully met Pete Reynolds at the airport. As usual, Pete was tinkering with some last-minute adjustments on his plane.

Pete shook his hand. “What are we looking for this time, Bo?”

“A wickiup along the edge of that meadow up on Boulder Creek.”

“Sounds reasonable,” Pete said. “What’s in it for me if we find it?”

“A thousand dollars.”

“Seems fair. “What’s in it for you?”

“Dinner at the Space Needle in Seattle.”